CITY OF WONDER

E. Charles Vivian

CENTAUR PRESS
Distributed by
COMO SALES, INC.
799 Broadway   New York 10003

CITY OF WONDER
Centaur Press edition, November 1973
Printed in the United States of America
SBN 0-87818-010-9

Cover illustration by David Ireland

Centaur Press Colophon:
Lawan Chomchalow

THE ROAD

Kir-Asa stands, <u>trebly</u> guarded, and most remotely secure of all the world's secret places since men began to make history, away in the wilds that still exist in certain lands of the Pacific. The way to Kir-Asa is guarded by savages who persist in the use of poisoned arrows, by snakes of the jungle, and the things of the wild that are fierce as the savages, stealthy as the snakes, and stronger than either savages or snakes.

If you would approach the barriers that guard Kir-Asa, you must come in a boat of shallow <u>draught</u> to a shore that is mud <u>unalloyed</u>. Then you get out from the boat with a rope to tow it to solid ground if you want it for the return journey, and flounder knee-deep across the flats over which the tide washes; later, you come to a belt of coarse grass beyond reach of the tides, where land-crabs run about; beyond this is scrubby bush, then open grassland, and then jungle-clad, gentle slopes—rise and fall, each ridge a little higher than the last, and then a long, slow descent to open, treeless marsh, where the waterfowl rise up in clouds at sight of a human form, and the mosquitoes swarm, <u>pestilentially</u>. It is three days' journey from the coast to the nearer edge of this marsh, two days more of weary travelling across the marsh, and then the thick jungle begins again.

That way came Watkins, Bent, and I, Faulkner. Watkins—so he told us at the outset—had the tale of Kir-Asa and various landmarks from an old, old Dyak who had travelled far in his time, and whom Watkins met up in British North Borneo. He had persuaded the tramp steamer's captain to bring us and our gear and our flat-bottomed boat down the coast, and to drop us off the mud shore—from the Dyak, he said, he had landmarks, which he would not describe to us, to bid him leave the steamer so as to strike the shore nearest to Kir-Asa.

As to food, we had no trouble either in the five days of dreary labour that took us to the jungle edge after

1

we had secured our boat well above high-water mark, or, in fact, at any time in the expedition, except for such as shall be told in its place. There were three or four species of antelope, and wildfowl without end, and we had two rifles and a double-barrelled shot-gun in addition to our revolvers. Also we were not much troubled as regards water; our chief preoccupations were those of warding off fever and possible roving savages, though of the latter we had little fear until we had got through the marshy belt. It was no country to attract even a savage, but a misery to travel through and a matter for relief when passed.

Before the heat grew to torture, the morning of the sixth day, the jungle edge showed like a wall before us. We paused in the slush of the marshland, gazing, and suddenly Watkins pointed at what looked like a sunken gully in the forest top.

"The road to Kir-Asa," he said.

It was as if, at that point, the jungle growth had failed, or as if it might at one time have been, as he said, a road, for though jungle creepers laced and twined there as elsewhere, there were no great trees—there was no evidence of heavy, monstrous forest growth such as luxuriated on either side of the road, or ravine, or whatever it might be. We floundered toward it, our boots squelching and sucking in the sodden marsh; all three of us were agueish, spent with the steamy damp of the last two days' travel, and sore from the bites of many insects. Yet we were all heartened when Watkins pointed—the tale told by his old Dyak held good, so far.

So we came to the fall in the level of the jungle roof, and, before we reached the edge of the jungle itself, found firm ground beneath our feet. I paused and, turning, called to the others to look back; we were on a ridge, or causeway, which ran arrow-straight across the marsh, raised above the level of the water-logged land.

"Aye," said Watkins, "the road to Kir-Asa. If we had struck it before, we'd have been here sooner."

In making up our equipment, he had put in three machetes with which one can slash through undergrowth, and now we found the need of these. By nightfall we had slashed our way about a mile into the

2

jungle, following that lightening of the growth and absence of great trees that made a continuation of the slight ridge or causeway across the marsh. We made a clearing, built and lighted a great fire, and so camped. My hands were a mass of blisters from the machete handle, and I was stiff and shivering with the fever from the marsh lands. Bent was but little better, but Watkins, tough pioneer that he was, seemed as happy here as when we had first met him, a year before, over in Java.

"Ah, you boys!" he said. "You'll harden off before you're through."

In the morning he pulled away creeper roots, and dug and fussed in the soft leaf mould down beside our fire, until he had a hole or pit six or seven feet deep—the stuff cleared away easily enough. At this depth he dug and dug with his machete point, flinging out earth and rotted vegetation until the machete struck and rang on something hard. With his hands he cleared a space about a yard square, or a little more, and, jumping down into the pit, we saw enough of his clearing to give us an idea of the nature of the road to Kir-Asa.

The little piece that he had uncovered was solid rock, laid in blocks of about a foot square that fitted diagonally to each other as one looked up or down the direction of the road—that is, the corners of the squares pointed up and down the direction in which we were travelling, and the sides of the blocks were diagonal to the line of the road. So perfect was the fitting of these blocks that a fine knife-blade could not have been inserted between them, and now we knew why only the lighter jungle creepers grew along the way. And this great work, we estimated, was not less than sixty feet in width.

I thought of the Forth Bridge, of the Pyramids, of St. Peter's at Rome, of New York's sky-scrapers; I called to mind the great architectural and engineering achievements of the world, and knew them all for pigmy trifles compared with the building of this tremendous causeway, so solidly laid that in unnumbered centuries the jungle that had hidden it could not conquer or break it. If the mere road was such titans' work, of what fashion must be Kir-Asa, to

3

which the road led?

In the lower jungle between the marsh and our camps, only the existence of this road, preventing the heavier jungle growth from taking root, made it possible for us to cut a way—to either side the forest was impenetrable, except for an organised expedition with adequate means for clearing. But, from the point of our camping, the way sloped upward, and as we went up the undergrowth thinned out until, save for slashing at a creeper here and there, we had free passage-way through the gloom of the forest. For still it was forest; where the moisture was not enough to nourish the rank undergrowth of the lowlands, still the soil would feed the more deeply rooted trees which crowded on each other to either side of us, while our causeway, buried as it was feet deep in leaf-mould, still refused to support heavy timber, and nurtured only saplings and rank tropic weed. Thus, the going having become easier, we made a dozen miles that day. An hour before nightfall we followed a game track into the wood on our right and found a drinking pool. Down by its edge Watkins cut a snake in half with his machete, just in time to save Bent's life—the snake was in the act of springing when the blade fell on it, and, had its fangs reached Bent, he would never have seen the sunset.

Having drunk our fill, and replenished our water-bottles, we went back to the causeway. There we built our fire, cooked our meal, and camped for the night.

"Why are we the first to come this way?" I asked Watkins, as we sat by our fire that night.

He looked at me with a slow, reflective smile on his lined face. "When I was in London," he answered, "I met a man who had lived there fourteen years and had never been inside St. Paul's Cathedral."

I pondered this while he smiled. A lean, spare little man, attractively ugly, who, if he travelled from Hong Kong through the Straits to Auckland, could speak the tongue of nearly every native he might meet on the way; who knew all the customs of the East, and nearly all its legends—a man who had little liking for civilisation, and a reputation for going on strange quests, like this of Kir-Asa. Such was Watkins, our leader and indeed our chief.

"I am not sure we are the first," he said.

"Who else, then?" Bent asked.

Watkins shook his head. "Past my telling, as yet," he answered.

We sat silent about the fire for awhile. Bent threw on the flame more of the dead wood we had collected.

"The Pacific is full of legends," Watkins said at last, "and the more one knows of native dialects, the more stories one hears. There's the sunken treasure of the Pahenge river, and the jewels of the ruined temple of Mah-Eng, and the lost ruby mine in the Firesi hills, and I know four different stories of buried pirate hoards. Nobody has ever been to look for these things, as far as I know. A legend grows up on a little less than nothing, and people distrust it."

Bent yawned sleepily. "How much farther have we to go?" he asked.

Watkins shook his head. "A day, a week, a month," he answered. "I don't know, and—does it matter? So long as game and water don't fail us—the old Dyak I got this story from could only tell me how to find the trace of the road at the edge of the jungle, by the sinking among the tree-tops—I'd heard of the existence of Kir-Asa before."

"What of it?" I asked.

"The oldest work of man left on earth," Watkins said.

"But——" Bent put in, and paused.

"Well," Watkins said, "our agreement was quite good enough for you when we made it—good pay for both of you for a year, or as much longer as the trip lasts, and twenty per cent apiece of any findings."

"What are the findings?" Bent asked rather irritably—in spite of quinine, he was still a little under the marsh fever.

"Kir-Asa, perhaps," Watkins said. "Jungle and old ruins, bare rock, gold, crumbled tombs, decay, nothing—Kir-Asa."

I had a feeling that he knew more than he cared to tell, though why, buried in the heart of the jungle, he should withhold from us any of the story that he knew, was more than I could guess.

I had met him, a year before, in Java, and had got to

know him and like him better as I knew him more. About a month before we landed on the mud flats he had put the proposition of this quest before me, telling me even less than he told now, but offering good pay, and a year's wage in advance if I accepted the proposal he made—which I was glad to do. Before he came to me, he had found and fixed up with Bent on terms similar to those he and I made. He had done all the organising, taken command and with a year's pay to my credit I had set out with him and Bent, content in the knowledge that my pay was awaiting me at the end of the venture, and perhaps more than mere pay. As to this latter, however, I knew nothing; I followed where Watkins led, and if the twenty per cent of findings materialised in any large way so much the better. Meanwhile, I went on with an easy mind, except when snakes were numerous, as they were at times in the jungle undergrowth.

THE ROAD ENDS

We came out, at about noon of the next day, through thinning growth to country resembling English park-land. There was rich, long grass, with scattered clumps of ancient trees, yet not so scattered that they did not hide the view at little more than a mile away from us. Our pocket aneroid gave us an elevation of four thousand feet, for the way had sloped upward in varying gradations since we left the marsh behind, and here the air was fresh and cool compared with the clammy heat of the lowlands behind us.

Still the trace of the mighty road guided us. The clumps of woodland, scattered about this park-like expanse, left clear a way that went straight as a stretched cord for miles, up to a rise beyond which showed a great smoke that went up to the sky and wavered and broke in the wind that set in steadily from the coast we had left. Here, as in the jungle, the road had become overgrown and buried in the centuries that had passed since men used it, but the mark of its builders remained in that no trees had been able to root themselves in its massive paving.

We trudged on till near on nightfall, and camped by a line of deeper green in the long grass, where a spring oozed up from among the roots of a great tree to trickle away and lose itself to southward. It was Bent, I think, who tempted fate by remarking that we were unusually lucky in meeting neither savages nor anything more disagreeable and dangerous than snakes. There was a yellowish-green, hooded kind of snake of which we had already killed nearly a dozen since entering the jungle, of which, Watkins told us, the bite was certain death. So far, it was our only enemy.

Not that the land was deserted—far from it. That night, as I lay by the fire, the noises of the wild kept me long awake. I heard Bent's placid breathing—he lay next to me, and Watkins beyond him—only at intervals for there was the squealing and chattering of monkeys not far off, and the many cries of settling birds, until it was quite dark. Later, there were grunts and roars and squealings—back toward the jungle we had left I heard the succession of noises that told how a tiger had made his kill, and until I went to sleep the bleating of antelope kids and the howls of jackals troubled the night. We were in a hunter's paradise, it seemed.

I wakened early, and dozed again till dawn. We had for covering a seven by six waterproof sheet apiece, with a lining of fleece. It was very light to carry, and in that climate quite enough for warmth as well as full protection from the heavy dews. Wakening fully when the day had come, I threw off my covering and sat up. Watkins was rubbing his eyes and yawning, but Bent lay on his back, very still.

I stared at him, wondering if it were an effect of the light that made his face seem so pale beneath the tan of exposure. Even his lips looked pale and bloodless, and there was a chalky appearance about his cheeks that normally were so healthily tinged beneath their tan. I leaned toward him, and his breathing was faint as an infant's.

"Bent!" I called. He did not stir. Watkins sat up on his side and leaned over the sleeper. I saw him pull back the collar of Bent's shirt and bend down close to his neck, and then he looked up at me.

"Get a fire going as soon as you can," he bade, speaking so as not to rouse Bent. "We must boil him

7

up some sort of soup—he's had his veins drained by a vampire bat."

I needed no second bidding, but had our tin can on a fire as quickly as possible, and chopped up a leg of buck that Watkins had shot the day before, to simmer and make soup. We left Bent to sleep until a rich liquid had simmered out from the meat, and then Watkins wakened him—he was weakly surprised at his own inability to sit up straight.

This, our first set-back, cost us three days. We rigged a sort of shelter for Bent, and, after the first day, gave him a twig to keep the flies off himself while we tended camp and amused ourselves as best we could. Watkins went searching vainly for a weed from which—so he said—he could make a tolerable substitute for tobacco, of which we had none left. I went shooting for the pot, an easy business, since the wild things here had never faced a gun before, and I think many of them had never even encountered man.

No incident of those days is worth record; on the morning of the fourth day we went on, Watkins and I carrying all Bent's gear, and even then our convalescent found it hard to keep pace with us. Two tiny punctures, already nearly healed, in the left side of his neck, were all that he had to show; had it not been for Watkins' knowledge of the cause of his weakness he might have died, for it was my first experience of such a danger as this, though I knew the country was not innocent of vampire bats.

I have said that, from where we camped, the trace of the ancient road led on to a rise that hid what lay beyond. On the fourth day, in spite of Bent's weakness, we went up to the crest of that rise and paused, for there the road ceased. There, it seemed, the way to Kir-Asa ended.

Abruptly, as we topped the rise a great gulf yawned before us, its brink less than a dozen paces from the crest of the long ascent. It ran transversely to the line of our approach, and the farther cliff was not less than a hundred yards distant from where we stood. I can think of no better simile for that tremendous gorge than that it was as if some giant had taken a colossal wedge and split the rock foundations of the world as a woodman might split a tree.

From behind us the westering sun shone on the upper part of the gulf's far wall; in the mother-rock were streaks of quartz and mica, so that the cliff looked like a mighty jewelled mosaic wrought by the hands of gods. To southward the chasm ran unbroken, precipice-walled, as far as eye could reach; to the north, it went to a horizon of tumbled, jagged rocks, from among which little pillars of smoke went up here and there. And beyond the cliff in front of us rose a heavier smoke pillar, the one we had seen for miles back along our way, though now as we stood at gaze the crater that sent it forth was still hidden by the great ravine's far edge.

Watkins went forward to the brink of the cliff and looked over—while he leaned and looked into the gulf my heart stood still, and I wanted to call out to him, but dared not speak. He turned and beckoned to me.

"Come and see what you think of it, Faulkner."

So I went, nine paces of the dozen walking and the other three on my hands and knees, for from where we had been standing the ground fell a matter of six feet or so, to the edge where Watkins stood so unconcernedly. I crawled to the edge.

"Hold my feet, Watkins," I asked.

He promptly sat on my calves, grinning in his infernally cool way, and, so secured, I got my head over the cliff edge and looked down. I saw that though at the top the walls of the chasm seemed perpendicular, yet the cleft appeared to narrow as it went down to a dimness where—I judged it somewhere between five and eight hundred feet—the daylight failed to penetrate. Yet, in spite of this impression—or illusion—of less width of cleavage in the depths, the rock face down which I looked went sheer away until lost in obscurity. And faint and far down I could hear the splash of running water, while it seemed to me that a mist clouded the darkness into which I gazed.

I drew back, and, Watkins releasing my legs, crawled up again to where Bent sat waiting the fruits of our investigation. Watkins followed me slowly, and glancing back at the gulf.

"What I want to know," Bent said peevishly, "is what breed of fool built a road like that to a hole like this."

9

Watkins pointed across to the farther cliff, and there at its edge a curved depression showed, like the hump of a macadamized road seen in section. It was opposite and corresponding with the trace of the way we had followed.

"This gulf has been made by an earthquake, or some convulsion, since the road was built," he said. "When the road was laid down it went straight westward from Kir-Asa to the coast. But our main problem isn't how the road was made—we have to join up with the other end of it over there—the problem is how to cross this." And, with a gesture, he indicated the great chasm that barred our way.

THE WRITING ON THE ROCK

Since Bent was still weak from loss of blood, we agreed to camp without trying to push on further that day. We had a drink and refilled our water-bottles at a spring three or four miles back—it was a trickle similar to that by which we had made our preceding camp. With nearly a quart of water apiece, and the cool of the evening coming, we counted ourselves safe as regards thirst, so we moved back about a quarter of a mile from the ridge to a clump of trees, and there built a fire to cook the half haunch of buck that remained to us for food. Watkins was much concerned about the absence of vegetable food, I remember.

"We shall all get scurfy and pimply and evil-tempered," he declared. "An unrelieved meat diet is simply damnation, and since we got out of the jungle we've had nothing else."

We had got our fire going, and chunks of the half haunch were grilling, when he made this announcement. I was bending over the fire, attending to the meat, and Bent lay a little way off, stretched at full length with his face upturned to the sky. It wanted then about half an hour of sunset as nearly as I could judge—Watkins had the only watch that would keep good time; mine had gone wrong down in the marshes and Bent's gained so that he was for ever setting it by Watkins'. Still, on a trip like this, the exact time was not of much consequence.

As I bent over the fire, something came past my ear—Pst!—into the heart of the flames. I saw Watkins leap for a rifle and work the bolt to drive a cartridge from magazine to barrel-chamber, and then he lifted the rifle and fired so closely past me that the explosion almost stunned me. Again he fired, and yet again, and then, still holding the rifle, he began to run.

It had all passed so quickly that he was charging past me before I had recovered from the shock of his first shot, and before Bent could get on his feet. When I had straightened myself and looked round, I saw two grotesque figures on the ground, about fifty yards away toward the great chasm, and Watkins was chasing a third who had nearly reached the crest of the ridge. Up there, at the edge of the ridge, this third figure turned as if awaiting its pursuer, with what looked like a slender stick raised to its face. Watkins, whom I knew to be a splendid shot with a rifle, stopped to fire again; the figure on the ridge tottered, dropped its stick, then turned and disappeared toward the chasm. Either its arm was broken by the shot, or else the shoulder blade was damaged, for as it turned its arm that had held the stick fell and dangled uselessly; that it could still take to flight in spite of the terrific shock such a wound must involve spoke volumes for the physique of these beings who had come on us.

I followed, as quickly as possible, with the second rifle, leaving Bent to his own inclinations—I confess to having a hope that, semi-invalid as he was, he would stay and look to the grilling of our steaks. Watkins disappeared over the crest of the ridge, and as I came up to sight of the chasm I heard his rifle bark again, but hollowly and faintly. In a few seconds an echo of the shot was flung back by the farther cliff, and then the two rock walls tossed the sound back and forth between themselves till it sounded like the rattle of marbles on a pavement, and finally died away. But of Watkins I could see nothing.

The point to which the figure he pursued had fled was three or four hundred yards to the left of that from which we had looked down into the depths. I went down gingerly from the ridge, and in fear and trembling lay flat and looked over. The mystery of

11

Watkins' disappearance explained itself at once: a little ledge, some eighteen inches or less in width, ran steeply down the cliff face, forming a sort of path; about thirty yards down that path Watkins was kneeling, looking into the depths as unconcernedly as if he looked out of a ground-floor window in a suburban villa.

"Hullow!" I called.

He looked up at me. "It's a hell of a way down," he called back. "I ought to have heard him crash when he bounced on the floor down there, but never a sound came back. Hold on—I'm coming up again."

I drew back from the edge and waited, but it was fully a quarter of an hour before he came up, looking very thoughtful. We went back together toward our fire, and I felt grateful to Bent for having, as I had hoped, stayed to see to the cooking. He explained later that we had the two rifles, and as far as he could see we were two to one, so he judged that in his weak state he would be of little use to us.

We two stopped beside the second of the wild men whom Watkins had shot—the one farthest from our fire. He was a being streaked with paint, with a necklace of bones, and a slender tube—a blowpipe—dropped beside the recumbent figure. One hand was twitching feebly, and as my shadow fell across the man his eyes opened and glared up at me. He spat out some sentence that sounded weakly fierce, and even as he spoke drew up his limbs in a final convulsion, and so died. I looked at Watkins.

"What did he say?" I asked.

Watkins shook his head. "I don't know the language," he confessed. "It isn't any dialect of the Pacific that I've ever heard—sounds more like a jargon derived from Aryan roots. I seemed to get two words—one was either 'vengeance' or 'expiation,' according to the context, and the other was 'ghosts' or perhaps 'shadows'—it may have been a curse at you because your shadow fell on him."

He prodded the corpse with his foot, indifferently, as if it had been that of a rat.

"We've had a narrow squeak," I said. "If it hadn't been for your marvellous shooting——"

"I knew we simply had to bag all three," he

12

answered, almost apologetically. "If that beggar I chased had got away, he might have brought a whole tribe down on us. Your escape, by the way, was a miracle. That arrow that went into the fire instead of into you would have put paid to your account in about ten minutes—these chaps all tip their arrows with the same sort of poison, no matter what dialect they speak. Let's go and get some grub, unless Bent has frizzled the steaks to cinders."

We went back to the fire, and saw as we passed that the other man, whom Watkins had shot first, was quite dead—the expanding bullet had taken him just under the eye, and, as is the way with that sort of ammunition, in its exit had blown the back of his skull away.

"After grub," Watkins said, "we'd better tumble these chaps over the cliff, or else the jackals will give us no sleep to-night."

It was a gruesome thought, but our appetites suffered not at all because of it. We polished off the meat, wiped our hands on the grass, had a sparing drink apiece from our water-bottles, and then Watkins and I lugged the two carcases to the top of the ridge and sent them rolling down. We agreed between ourselves, now that human enemies had put in an appearance, that it was not enough protection merely to keep up a good fire. Between us we would keep four-hour watches, letting Bent sleep the night through, since he had not completely recovered from his loss of blood. We spun a knife for choice of watches, and Watkins calling "Point!" won, since the knife came down handle first. Then we went back to our fire, and threw into it the little satchels of poisoned arrows and the blowpipes, which we had not sent over the cliff with the bodies of their owners. There were a couple of spears which we let lie where they had fallen, half-hidden in the grass.

I settled down beside Bent, who slept soundly, as Watkins had elected to take the first watch. It was then hardly dark, and though the day had been tiring enough sleep was not for me. I could see Watkins sitting with the firelight on him, gazing toward the ridge; as I watched him, he got up and paced back and forth restlessly—he seemed, from what the glow of the fire showed me of his face, perplexed over some problem, for he frowned and shook his head at times.

So he alternated between sitting and pacing up and down until moonrise, and then I must have dozed. The moon was but a little way up from the horizon when he wakened me to take my turn at watching.

Our precaution, though wise, proved needless, for nothing more came to disturb us. Our fire kept off jackals and other prowling beasts, and the three wild men Watkins had killed had no followers, as far as we were concerned. When it was time I roused Watkins again, and this time slept without difficulty until after sunrise.

And there sat Watkins, frowning as he gazed into the fire. He looked at me and smiled as I sat up.

"I've been thinking," he announced. "Last night, chasing that savage, I found what I came to find, and now I'm wondering whether to go on or turn back."

I stared, wondering at his words. In the end he laughed.

"I'm quite sane," he said. "Down that ledge there's a sort of cave or recess in the rock. In the cave there are some bones and an inscription scratched on the rock."

"Well?" I asked, mystified not only at the existence of a readable inscription in such a spot as this, but at its possible connection with the man before me.

"You asked, some days ago," he said deliberately, "about our being first to come this way, and I told you I was not sure about our being first. I had an idea that a relative of mine had preceded us, and last night I found all that was left of him. But what he's left—what he scrawled on the rock, makes me curious, and I feel inclined to go on, down the cliff."

"Down that ledge?" I asked incredulously.

He nodded. "It's not nearly so bad as it looks."

Now—it is a weakness that I share with most men I believe—I hated to confess that I was horribly afraid even of looking over the cliff, but it seemed that the alternatives lay between confession of my fears and actually setting foot on that perilously narrow ledge. Mentally, I postponed the confession.

"I suggest that you come and see the statement of my ancestor, so as to assure yourself that I'm not guying you," Watkins said. "And then we can come back, tell Bent, and decide whether to go on or to go back. It won't take more than half an hour, and we can leave Bent to sleep until we get back here."

Sitting comfortably there by the fire, well out of sight of those tremendous cliffs, I had a sudden access of courage. I told myself that if Watkins could crawl about that cliff like a fly going down a wall, I'd be hanged if I wouldn't screw myself up to doing likewise.

"Right," I said, and I fancy the ready acceptance of his proposal surprised him, since he must have known when he sat on my legs what it meant to me even to look down into the gulf. "Let's start now." For I wanted to get it over before my fit of bravery evaporated.

So we set out. By screwing up my resolution I managed to keep on my feet when we got to the brink of the cliff, and Watkins, preceding me, gave me a hand until I was safely on the sloping ledge that made so dizzy a pathway.

"Don't look down," he bade—needlessly enough, for I dared not. "Keep your eyes on where your feet must tread, and try and think of any funny stories you know."

But all I could get in my mind was that, to be gramatically correct, he should have said "try to think," not "try and think." I was about to tell him this when we came to the cave or recess of which he had spoken. It was a cleft like an inverted V with a flat floor on which was a confusion of bones—a skull among them, minus the lower jawbone—and some rusted bits of metal, including the barrel and trigger mechanism of what I took to be an old muzzle-loader. There was, too, a rusty, bone-handled knife, and there were some mouldering rags, and a couple of bone buttons. Here some civilised man had come to his end.

Watkins, without speaking, pointed at the right-hand wall as we faced inward to the cleft, and I read what had been scratched—I judged with some metal implement—in the soft rock. I transcribe the message from the pencilled copy that Watkins made then and there:

"RECORD CONCERNING IOHN WATKYNS, HERMANN ROEDERER, CORNELIUS VAN VUUREN, DIRK VAN DEN

HEUVEL, PETER SLUYS, AUTOMN 1768. IN APRIL 1766 WE FIVE CAME SEARCHING FOR Kir Asa. PETER SLUYS WAS BIT BY A SERPENT IN THE FOREST AND WE BERIED HIM. BY GODD HIS MERCY WE PASSED THE TREMBLING BRIDGE THAT IS IN THIS GULPH AND CLIMBED TO THE PLACE WHERE GHOSTS CHASE WOMEN. SO IT IS NAMED. ALSO WE PASSED NANTIA THE WOMAN WHO RULES MONKEYS AND FOR MONTHS WERE PRISONERS IN THE LAND OF Kir Asa BEYOND THE WALL. THIS YEAR BEING FREED WE FLEDD AND RETURNED TAKING NOTHING OF THE PLACE BUT GLADD OF OUR LIVES.

"HERMAN ROEDERER AND DIRK VAN DEN HEUVEL WERE TORN IN PIECES OF THE MONKEYS RULED BY NANTIA. CORNELIUS VAN VUUREN ATE OF FISH HE CAUGHT IN THE RIVER THAT IS DOWN IN THE GULPH AND DIED MISERABLY AND I BERIED HIM. I IOHN WATKYNS HAVE CRAWLED HITHER FROM THE GULPH HAVING BROKEN MY LEGG BY THE ANKEL AFTER THAT I HAD PASSED THE TREMBLING BRIDGE. MY POWDER IS SPENT AND MY STRENGTH AND HERE I SHALL DIE COMMENDING MY SOUL TO MY MAKER.

"TO ANY WHO FOLLOW SEEK OUT PHILIP WATKYNS OR SEND HIM MESSAGE TO CLIFFE BY ROCHESTER IN KENT THAT IS IN ENGLAND TO TELL HIM HIS BROTHER IOHN MET DEATH WITH XTIAN FORTITUDE FOR I KNOW THAT HERE I DIE ALONE. AND IF YOU FOLLOWING FOLLOW TO Kir Asa KILL NANTIA WHO RULES MONKEYS. I COMMEND MY SOUL TO GODD THOUGH MY BODDY WILL BE TORN OF BEASTS FOR HERE I DIE ALONE NOT HAVING POWDER OR STRENGTH TO FACE THE WILD BEESTS THAT ROAM THE PLAIN AND WITH NOUGHT MORE TO EAT. IOHN WATKYNS OF CLIFFE BY ROCHESTER IN KENT."

Watkins finished his transcription, kneeling to read what was inscribed near down to the ground. I picked up the rusty knife and saw how, apart from corrosion, its point was worn down. With this for tool, "Iohn Watkyns" had inscribed his story on the stone, and the awful fate that the story pictured appalled me. Somehow this iron-nerved man had dragged himself up from the "gulph" with a broken ankle, and here he had set himself to make this record in the knowledge that, foodless and disabled, he must wait here until pain and starvation left a lifeless body for the jackals.

"Here I die alone." I pictured him, sending his thoughts across to the home at "Cliffe by Rochester" and waiting "with Xtian fortitude" for the inevitable end, in the certainty that no help could reach him. In presence of the evidence of a tragedy so grimly pathetic I had little thought for Kir-Asa and what the inscription told of the way there. The man himself, scrawling his message on the rock as he waited for death to find him, occupied all my mind then, and I seemed to see him sitting here, his message finished, looking out to the grim rock wall across the chasm and in fancy recalling the faces he would never see again. The awful, final isolation that the message conveyed, the doomed man's unassuming courage in a situation so utterly devoid of hope, made up such a depth of tragedy as I had never before imagined.

Watkins, taking off his coat and spreading it on the floor of the cave, began picking up the bones that lay scattered about and placing them on the coat. I gave him a hand, and when we had them all picked up he took up the coat.

"Let's get back," he said. "This was a brave man, and we'll do him all the honour we can by burying his remains decently. We can talk about his message outside—I don't feel like it, here."

"Neither do I," I confessed. And so, Watkins carrying the bones wrapped in his coat, we made our way up to the top of the cliff. But, either because of the deep impression made on me by the writing in the cave, or because a danger faced is never so great as a danger anticipated, I thought far less of walking up the ledge that had cost me so much resolution to descend.

WE HOLD A COUNCIL

The bones that had been "Iohn Watkyns" were decently and reverently buried at a little distance from the top of the cliff, and we three sat round the ashes of our fire, which we had let die down. Watkins had intimated to Bent that he wished to have a talk before moving on, and Bent and I sat waiting while he arranged in his own mind what he wished to say and discuss. At last he began:

"When I bargained with you two," he said, "I told you that my object was hunting and exploration, and that I had a yarn from an old Dyak about Kir-Asa. That was all true, but it was not all the truth. Back there where men are plentiful I had no wish to tell more than would get me two good men as companions on a trip like this, because—well, apart from all else, Kir-Asa may be worth finding."

Here he paused. I saw that Bent, nursing his knees, rested his chin on them and looked hard at Watkins. He had grown very silent since the incident of the vampire bat, and it seemed to me that he was hardly as grateful as he might have been for the consideration—even solicitude—that Watkins showed him.

"Now," Watkins went on, "I've always had a liking for antiquities, and stories of strange places, but it was not till my father died that I had any opportunity of indulging my likings—I earned my own living from Darjeeling to Hong-Kong, and from there to Penang, and pretty much all over the islands. That's not the story, though. Away at my home there's a faded old manuscript diary that my grandfather's great-grandfather kept. There's not much in it of interest concerning him—his name was Philip Watkins, and he lived at a place called Cliffe, in north Kent."

"It seems to me," Bent said, "that you're merely telling family history. I mean—this hardly concerns us."

Watkins looked across at him. "When you're a little older, and a little wiser, Bent," he said coldly, "you'll also be a little more patient. I'm not telling these details without reason—they link up with the grave we dug and the bones we buried—while you were resting—an hour or two ago."

"Oh, well," Bent said carelessly, "I apologise. Go on."

"Bent," Watkins said, and the word sounded like the snap of a steel trap. "I don't take apologies that veil mere contempt or lack of interest. What I have to say involves a decision as to whether we go on or go back from here. I'm talking with a purpose, not to develop my lungs."

There was some hint of the latent power in the man as he fixed and beat down Bent's gaze. I found my admiration of him growing yet more—it had been growing all the way from the coast.

"I'm sorry," Bent said, with more of reality in the words, "and—I'm listening."

"But Philip Watkins' diary," Watkins went on after a pause for thought, "had one interesting portion, which told of a brother, John Watkins, who came home from service with the old John Company, and brought back a story of a place called Kir-Asa. I'm not going to detail that story to you two now—it's too incredible. But, on the strength of the story, John borrowed five hundred pounds from his brother and came east again. Here he either hired or took into partnership four Dutchmen, and Philip got a letter giving the names of the four and saying they were starting with John from Batavia. And that was the last Philip ever heard of his brother.

"When I came East, I brought the knowledge of John's starting out, and brought in my mind all he had told Philip of the nature of the adventure he contemplated. But it was not till a little over a year ago that I could get any mention of a place called Kir-Asa anywhere, and then I came on an old Dyak—you both know that part of the story. His directions brought us here, and less than a mile from here, Bent, I found the end of the story of John Watkins, together with his bones—Faulkner knows it. It was scratched on the side of a cave in which John Watkins died, and I'll read it out as I copied it in the cave this morning."

He read the pathetic inscription very slowly, and Bent listened intently. As he paused at the end, Bent put in:

"And now you intend to decide whether to finish here or go on?"

"Not yet," Watkins answered. "I intend first to weigh up this message sentence by sentence, discuss it thoroughly, and then take the opinion of you two as to what we ought to do, though I think I'm pretty fully decided myself, already. But if you two don't agree—if you're both of one mind against me—well, it's too serious and perhaps dangerous a matter for any but a majority decision to take us on."

19

He took up the copy of "Iohn Watkyns" record again and studied it. "First of all," he said, "assuming that we go on, we've got to get through that cleft in the earth—up and down the cliffs. We can save ourselves the trouble of searching for any other route—John Watkins and his party must have searched both ways of the cleft to see if they could get round it before going the way they did, and that's the best, if not the only way. Agreed?"

"Agreed," I said, and: "Assuming that we go on," Bent remarked.

"We can tackle the trembling bridge, and what he calls 'the place where ghosts chase women,' when we come to them, as the record does not describe them in any way that would help us in preparing ourselves. Thus we needn't discuss them till we know a little more about them. Agreed?"

To this we both assented, without hesitation or comment.

"As for Nantia and her monkeys, old age has probably done her in and saved us any trouble, but it strikes me as a sort of guard over the place that may have been replaced or kept up—a big danger. That control of animals, when it exists among savages, runs in families and is generally handed down, and there's nothing more terrible to face than a troop—or whatever the collective word is—of big monkeys. It's something to watch and save revolver ammunition for, but since John's party got through without damage, one way, with far less efficient equipment than breech-loading pistols, I don't see why we shouldn't get through."

"If we go on, I agree," Bent said.

"All this is assuming that we do go on," Watkins said calmly, though I could see that the calm hid irritation. "Now, beyond the monkeys, the party that preceded us were taken prisoners, but were not harmed. That stamps the people who took them prisoners as something more than ordinary savages, who usually kill their prisoners after more or less torture—there's a hint of trouble in their being glad to get away with their lives, but they did get away. Further, as I read it, they left behind something that would have been worth bringing with them—'taking nothing of the place'—the record states, showing that there was something to take."

He paused and looked at us questioningly. We both nodded assent.

"As to the disasters of the return journey, we can't blame Kir-Asa for them," he suggested.

"I conclude Nantia's monkeys belong to Kir-Asa," I said, "and if so Kir-Asa is to blame."

"If we go on," he said, "we shall find out about that. Now, as to whether we go on or no, I've summed up all the record tells us. For myself, I think we're forewarned to a certain extent, and there's a chance of making good over our findings. At the worst, we shall probably have as good a chance of getting away as the party before us, and at the best we may come back very rich men. And—I hate giving up a thing once I've begun it."

"Watkins," I asked, "what is Kir-Asa?"

"I know very little," he answered frankly. "Philip's diary that I spoke of—you must remember that it was written about a century and a half ago—tells the fantastic tales that came from the East in those days. But I judge it to be a very old city or place, Atlantean, perhaps, or even a survival from Lemuria, the continent that was before Atlantis. It may be just a relic of an Eastern state only a few hundred years old, though what we saw of the surface of the road points to something far greater. By what Philip's diary tells, there are traces of Lemuria about the place—uncanny traces—but what he wrote, which is what his brother told him, may be only travellers' tales. As to what Kir-Asa is, my own inclination is to go and find out."

"And mind," Bent said slowly, "is exactly the reverse."

"Well," Watkins commented, "perhaps you're wise. But since you're the youngest member of the party, and volunteered your decision before Faulkner had a chance to speak, perhaps you'll state your reasons fully."

"I believe," Bent said, choosing his words with care, "that your ancestor was rather delirious with pain from his broken leg when he cut that record in the rock. His story of a place where ghosts chase women, and a woman who could rule a herd of monkeys, goes a long way beyond probability. He says nothing definite about anything at Kir-Asa to make the expedition worthwhile, and I don't like the idea of risking my neck on those cliffs, since there's no avoiding them if we go on, without some better prospect of a real profit accruing. It looks to me like a series of grave dangers for the sake of what you yourself have owned may be only travellers' tales."

"There's one bit of evidence to the contrary that I haven't mentioned," Watkins said, "and that's the sentence spoken by the man I shot last night—you remember, Faulkner, when your shadow fell on him. It was nothing like the ordinary dialects of the Pacific, and it pointed to the existence in these parts of a totally different kind of race. In the same way as my ancestor's imprisonment without harm of any kind points to the existence of some sort of civilisation, as distinct from the savage sort of life you generally find about this quarter of the world."

"Proves nothing, with regard to Kir-Asa," Bent said doggedly. "Apart from the bit of road you uncovered, there's no real evidence."

Watkins turned toward me. "Faulkner—the casting vote?" he asked.

I think he knew what it would be. "I'm for going on," I said. "If you turned back now, I should be for ever hungering to come along this road again and find out what it was that we had missed."

After this there was a long silence between us, broken in the end by Bent. "Well," he said, "what shall we do about it?"

There was a hint of obstinancy in the manner of the question, as if he feared coercion and would resist it. Watkins considered his words very carefully in replying.

"Bent," he said, "when we started on this trip you knew quite well it was no week-end excursion to a seaside resort, but a difficult and possibly dangerous task. I gave you to understand that much, as I did with Faulkner—when I bargained for your services. For my part I looked to get two sound men who would follow through any hells there are to reach our objective."

"You yourself have owned that the objective is not only vague," Bent interrupted, "but quite possibly non-existent. It's a quest of shadows."

"And does that matter two halves of a damn to you, under the terms of our agreement?" Watkins asked, suddenly exploding out of his usual calm. "On a trip like this anything short of absolute concord may spell disaster at any minute—one must lead, and it is for the others to fall in with the leading, so long as it's fair and just. Your attitude breaks the concord, spoils leading. The fact that I, the leader, think it better to go on than to leave the possibilities unexplored ought to be enough for you, if what you said when you agreed to come counts for anything."

"Frankly," Bent said, "I don't like the look of the thing. It's as I said, a quest of shadows, a maximum of risk with a minimum possibility of profit."

"Look here," Watkins suggested. "Subject to Faulkner's approval, we two will come back with you through the jungle to the edge of the marsh, back down to the low country where we began to cut a way. You can take either the shot-gun or a rifle, make your way to the coast, and take the boat—you can work it on your own easily enough, and we'll find a way to get off the coast when the time comes for us to want one. That lets you out, we two can go on, and everybody's satisfied."

Whether the proposal shamed Bent or whether he feared to cross the marsh alone, I do not know. But he shook his head.

"No," he said, "the voting was two to one, and I abide by it. I merely stated my objections, and my views, but they're overruled. With me it's more a premonition of no good to come out of it than anything else—I'll come with you to Kir-Asa."

Watkins reached out his hand, and Bent took it.

"I'm glad we've talked it out and cleared the air," Watkins said. "We can only tackle a problem like this in absolute agreement—there must be no divided opinions about it. And now it's settled—we go on."

We decided to make a day on the plain, shooting and cutting up for the pot, since it was pretty evident that the chasm would provide nothing in the way of food, and we did not know if it would take hours or days to reach the top of the farther cliff. At noon, when the sun shone directly into the cleft, Watkins and

I went and looked over the cliff edge; we saw, down in the depths, tumbling masses of pearl-grey cloud which hid the floor of the ravine and prevented us from making any estimate of its depth, and again we could hear faintly the sound of water falling. Beyond these things, our scrutiny added nothing to our knowledge of what we had to face. We knew that John Watkins had crawled up the cliff face to the little cave, if his "record" told truth, while we ourselves had found a way down from the cliff edge to the cave. There was our path—no need to search for another.

Next morning, well stocked with cooked meat, we were ready to face the descent of the cliff.

THE TREMBLING BRIDGE

Thinking over the inscription in the cave, as I lay wakeful at dawn of the morning when we were to begin our descent of the cliff, I divided the obstacles between us and Kir-Asa into three definite barriers. There was, first and nearest, the trembling bridge, whatever that might be; then came the "place where ghosts chase women," which would not have induced mention in John Watkins' record merely through the grotesqueness of the name, but was put down as something to be passed or overcome. And, lastly, there would quite possibly be the descendants of Nantia's monkeys.

I thought it all out, lying there while the sun rose. First, there was a natural obstacle, a bridge that involved some sort of danger; then came an appeal to the very instinct of fear, some psuedo-supernatural trickery, and then, if we held on resolutely beyond this, a tussle with the most dangerous form of wild beasts. And, having passed these three guarding factors, the intending visitor—assuming that conditions had not changed in the last century and a half—must reckon on being taken prisoner by way of welcome.

My meditations induced me to view Bent's objections leniently. I was no nearer to agreeing with him, but I could make allowance for his point of view. Then Watkins sat up, breathing forth threatenings and slaughter against the whole mosquito tribe. They were

24

not plentiful here, but apparently one had buzzed near enough to his ear to waken him.

"What's amusing you?" he asked, with some asperity, observing my smile.

"Partly language, and partly whiskers," I said.

"Well," he remarked thoughtfully, "I know I'm not exactly a replica of the Apollo Belvedere, at the best, but you're not quite so beautiful as you were, you know."

He ignored my comment on his wonderful flow of epithets—I had never before heard so many titles bestowed on a mosquito at one sitting. For the rest, he had added a fortnight's scrub of beard to his normal ugliness—for there is no disguising the fact that, even at his best, he was an ugly man. Squab nosed, and with a chin that gave no hint of his strength of character, just as his flat chest and rather sloping shoulders concealed great physical strength, he looked monkeyish, sitting there, for he was one of whose good qualities his friends had to learn; he displayed none on first acquaintance.

He handed me his little pocket mirror as a sort of suggestion, and it showed me a bristly chin, with a pimple or two, and plenty of dirt overlaying the tan on my face—none of us had washed since early in the preceding afternoon. I agreed with him that I was not in a fit state to indulge in criticisms.

Bent sat up as I returned the mirror. "Well," he remarked, "you're a pretty pair, anyway."

He wondered at our laughter. Away from the fellowships of normal life, it took very little to amuse us.

We made up the fire and breakfasted. Packing our limited belongings had become an automatic business, and when it was over we faced east. It seemed, that morning, as if all our journey had been a mere introduction. There was a sense almost of solemnity about our setting out, and I remember turning to look back at the park-like, grove-spotted level of the plain, bathed as it was in the brilliant light of early morning, and mentally bidding good-bye to the normal world. I think some similar feeling affected the others, for they too looked back and then set out without a word.

A little way on toward the ridge at the brink of the

cliff, Watkins paused and picked up the broad-bladed spear of the savage he had shot. For two nights it had lain there unheeded in the grass; now he held it out toward me.

"Ever seen anything like that before?" he asked.

I took the spear by its shaft and looked closely at the blade. As I had last seen it, fresh dropped from its owner's hand, the dullness of the metal had led me to take it for the average native workmanship on poor quality steel, a thing with little temper except at the point, quite ordinary in pattern. But now I saw that the two nights of exposure to dew had not produced the red ruse which one would expect to find; the metal had tarnished, and such slight traces of corrosion as it showed were more greenish than red.

"It's a nickel-copper alloy, or maybe tin or zinc," I said. "I'm no metallurgist."

"Neither am I," Watkins answered, "but the man who used this didn't trade in the bazaars of the coast towns. And, judging by the edge and the heft of the thing, they have a pretty taste in metals and the working of them where he came from."

"Copper-zinc alloy, well tempered, most probably," Bent put in, after looking closely at the blade.

I was about to drop the spear, but changed my mind. My rifle was slung on my back, military fashion, and this would form a sort of staff.

"May as well take it along," I remarked. "It might be useful, some time."

"Quite so," Watkins agreed. "In the same way, we might have brought along a few tree trunks, just in case we find ourselves running short of firewood."

We crossed the ridge at the point opposite to where the ledge ran down the cliff face to the cave, and Watkins led the way down the short slope to the very edge. Before setting foot on the path which led to the cave of "Iohn Watkyns," and beyond it we knew not where, he unslung his rifle—it would have been difficult on account of his pack, to get the weapon free for use in case of need on the cliff path, unless this widened beyond the cave. I was about to follow his example, but he stopped me.

"If the path widens," he said, "there'll be plenty of room for you to get your gun loose. If it doesn't widen, only the front man of the party can shoot with safety."

"That reminds me," Bent said. "Those three savages you shot must have come this way, surely."

"They may have come any way," Watkins answered.

"That breed travels miles on the hunt, in parties of anything between two and a dozen. The spearhead points to their having come this way, though, as does the fact that one of them tried to escape down the cliff—though with regard to that, he may have just known of this ledge and thought I might be afraid to follow down it. The bones in the cave might easily make the path taboo."

With that he went on, stepping over the cliff edge to the perilous path as unconcernedly as one might step out of a doorway on to a city pavement. I followed more cautiously, and metamorphically held my breath lest I should shake the cliff.

Once over the edge, I turned to see if Bent needed a hand, realising that he had not yet seen the way we had to travel. Bent stepped down, I think, without realising what he was facing. Then he must have looked down into the depths.

"O Lord!" he ejaculated, "I'd no idea it was like this."

"It isn't, really," I said, wonderfully strengthened in courage by the knowledge that somebody else was scared. "Keep your eyes on the path for footing—don't look down, and you'll find it easy enough."

We stopped at the cave, that Bent might see the record "Iohn Watkyns" had left. The rusty knife and the old gun barrel still lay there, together with the bone buttons and rags of clothing.

"If the savages know this path, how is it that these things were not taken away?" Bent asked, after he had read the inscription.

"I conclude," Watkins said, "that the path is used only at very rare intervals—it's not exactly the sort of road you'd use for a Sunday-school treat. The dead bones might have made the cave taboo, or else the things had rusted and rotted themselves useless before anyone came."

He led the way out again. "Anyhow," he said as he

27

went, "if it hadn't been for those savages we should probably have missed the existence of this path, and of the inscription."

We followed him gingerly downward. The sun had climbed high enough to light the ravine to a considerable depth, and at the outset we had no difficulty of any kind—the path, though nerve-shaking enough, was at the same time of such a width that one could walk on it as long as one refrained from looking into the depths. The slope was not too steep for safety, and for a matter of four hundred paces or so we simply walked, thus dropping probably sixty or eighty feet below our starting point. Here, however, the ledge narrowed to less than twelve inches in width, and became level; I heard Bent, behind me, give a little moan of fear, but dared not turn my head toward him. Watkins, from in front, called back "Stop" and I halted. Bent came up close to me and put a hand on my shoulder. I could feel him trembling.

"The path reverses here," Watkins said to me over his shoulder, "and I come back down under you. Don't move till I've passed you, and take the turn one at a time."

It was, as he said, a definite reversal of direction. The trace of the ledge on the side of the cliff was like the letter V laid on its side, and we were now at the point of the V. Watkins' head went past my waist as we two stood hugging the rock, and then I stepped forward, turned cautiously, and followed him at the lower level. Bent in his turn moved forward, turned, and came on down the reversed path.

There were either nine or ten of these reversing points on that crazy track, which must have been cut for the use of people with stronger nerves than ours. It took us down from sunlight to shadow, and ever the sound of falling water grew, until it was a steady roar in the confines of the chasm. The last reversing point brought us down to the level of thin, wreathing vapour, down to that point the path had given foothold on clean solid rock—so near to the vertical was the cliff, and so smooth its surface, that from the summit to the level of this thin mist there was no sign of vegetation, but now the surface of the ledge, on which we must keep foothold, grew moist with a greenish, fungus-like coating, something like that which covers stones on a shore down near low-water mark, but fortunately not quite so slippery.

To that point, I had no doubt that the greater part of the ledge had been cut by human agency, perhaps by the builders of the great road, and perhaps by succeeding inhabitants of this land. Here and there a bit of natural inequality in the cliff face may have been utilised to save labour, but the steady angle of descent, together with the presence of the reversing points, proved the use of tools—and what a stupendous, age-long task it must have been, this of making a way to replace the broken road! I pictured a race at the height of its power, cutting this track in preparation for the making of a safe, wide roadway, and dying out before the task was completed, or being extinguished suddenly by catastrophic overthrow, conquest or disease, perhaps.

I have spoken of our coming to the point where the thin mist began as if it were a mere stepping down a slope, but it was far more. There were narrowings of that dizzy path where even Watkins clawed his way, face inward to the cliff and arms outstretched, the unslung rifle that he carried scraping on the stone. And at these points I went breathlessly and in deadly fear lest the next step should send me down to the invisible depths, until, by reason of successive strains of this kind, I got past fear to a sort of numb indifference. At times I heard Bent make that sort of moaning sound with which he had first evinced his realisation of the nature of our journey, and at one or two of the reversing stations I saw his face, chalk-white with fright—my own could not have been greatly different. Only the steady nerve of Watkins, leading the way and giving us an example of unflinching courage, rendered the descent possible; we two could never have got down alone.

Near the top the rock was reddish grey, streaked with dark lines that bespoke the presence of iron, and with here and there interminglings of quartz and what I took to be signs of mica. Lower down, we came to a thick layer of copper pyrites—recognised by the golden gleam in the stone—and under that was a thick stratum of quartz resting on a still thicker layer of chalk.

Beneath that again was a flinty-looking kind of rock, almost agate-coloured and slightly transparent, pitted small-pox-fashion with tiny holes. These I remember, as well as a slanting vein of pumice-like rock, feet thick, which showed by its angle how volcanic action had at some time forced a channel through the earth-crust. There were other layers, including much of whitish, sparkling quartz—it was an object lesson in the making and settlement of the world's foundations, until at last we came to the unvarying green where the mist began.

It was then late afternoon, and we were all very hungry and very tired, but there was as yet no width of track on which we could rest. We went down into increasing dimness, and suddenly Watkins, with an "Ah!" of intense relief, stepped into such a recess as that in which we had found the bones, near the summit.

"We can rest and eat here," he said.

But first we drank, deeply, of our stores of water. Then, seated on the damp rock, we ate in the dimness. Here the roaring of water came to us as a great, persistent noise, over which we must raise our voices to make each other hear. We rested for half an hour or so, and the light neither diminished nor increased; I was for staying at this point for the night, since the cave gave ample and safe sleeping room, but Watkins elected to go on.

"We can't find damper accommodation, and I'd rather get to level," he said. "Besides, we've nearly finished our water, and there's plenty down there—I'd rather finish the descent before we get thirsty again."

Thus we took to the path, which slanted steadily for another hundred feet of descent, and at that point Watkins was a mere ghost in the fog only three or four yards in front of me. Here, however, the ledge suddenly doubled its width, and I closed up on him; the surface grew irregular, as if natural rather than hewn, and we came on transverse fissures, some of them quite wide enough to trap an unwary foot.

"Go carefully," Watkins called back to us. "This must have been where my ancestor broke his ankle, though how he ever made his way to the top with it broken is a miracle."

30

Over that I wondered, and wonder still. Yet hope will carry a doomed man far, and probably the fear of falling off the ledge drove "Iohn Watkyns" up and up until he reached the shelter of the cave in which he died.

By this time the thunder of the invisible waters was almost deafening and quite near us. The mist wreathed and eddied in a current of air that swept along the gorge from south to north, so that at times there were tantalising half-glimpses of the rocks before and beneath us, and then again we were enveloped in the roky, clammily warm whiteness of the fog curtain, through which our leader steadily groped his way.

We came suddenly to a level floor, boulder strewn; there was no longer a visible edge to the path toward the centre of the chasm, and the sound of falling water was very near indeed. The quality of the fog told us that it was still day overhead, and its whiteness made an unnatural, ghostly clearness of objects seen near at hand, though when the swirling masses thickened round us it was impossible to see clearly at a distance of six feet. Thus a boulder would seem to jump out of the reek as we came to it, and as suddenly would vanish behind, until, still following the line of the cliff, we found our way barred by a smooth, slanting wall of rock, down which trickles of water had worn tiny gullies.

Here Watkins turned at right angles, toward the centre of the chasm, though by this time the roar of the waters had grown so loud and obviously near that it seemed as if one more step would drop him into the invisible torrent. Suddenly he stopped, and I came abreast of him.

"The trembling bridge," he shouted, his lips close to my ear.

I peered forward, and in a momentary thinning of the mist saw that a great sheet of water poured over the slanting wall on our left, and fell, apparently far below the level of our feet, to the channel which the underground river had cut for itself in the floor of this mighty cleft. How deep the fall might be, or what was the width of the river, I could not tell, but the thunder of the cataract was majestic, its volume enhanced by the prisoning walls on either side.

Directly in front of the falling waters a mighty boulder, roughly oval in section, formed a bridge across the yawning gulf into which the waters fell. I can best describe it by saying that it was as if a slightly flattened torpedo had been placed with one end resting on each bank, only this torpedo was of stone, irregularly shaped, and with a sort of wing or fin projecting toward the waterfall from its main substance. On this projecting fin a portion of the waters of the cataract fell, and, as the underside of the stone bridge was oval in section, the whole fabric perpetually rocked and trembled as the water falling on the projecting fin upset its balance. It was an unending fight between the waterfall and the balanced stone; the weight of water eternally sought to roll the great boulder in toward the face of the falls, and the boulder itself as perpetually regained its balance and held itself away, being bedded in a slight depression at either end so that it could not turn over. The top of this trembling rock was about four feet in width, and at a level with my chest; I could not see it all, and could only tell vaguely what it was that caused the perpetual rocking and trembling; even when the swirling vapours were at their thinnest, only about eight or ten feet of this terrifying bridge were visible. Whether beyond, in the obscurity of the mist, the surface was sufficiently flat to admit of our crossing we could not tell. We knew only that, according to his record, "Iohn Watkyns" and his companions had made the crossing—but that was a century and a half ago. Though the years had not worn away the projecting fin enough to stop the trembling and rocking movement, there was no telling what the water had done to the surface of the boulder in that period.

Bent saw the bridge, and I saw both anger and fear on his face. My mind went back to his protesting decision.

"Do you think you're going to cross that?" he bellowed at Watkins.

"I know I am," Watkins roared back.

Bent shook his head, and half turned away irresolutely.

"Cross it, or go back up there alone and be damned to you!" Watkins yelled at him. And to that Bent made no reply.

Watkins stepped to where a trickle of water came down the rock wall at the cataract's edge, made a cup of his hands, and held them into the trickle. At the touch of the water he almost jumped back—it was the first time I had seen him so startled as to give more than normal sign of surprise. I went up and put out a hand, and the water was hot—not boiling, but past mere warmth; one could drink it with ease, as presently we did, but still it was hot. Somewhere higher up in its course this river came through an actively volcanic area, emerging from it as from some gigantic boiler, and now we knew why mist filled the lower levels of the gorge.

Without further speech Watkins made for the trembling bridge, and, as a boy might leap to gain the summit of a stone wall, with a jump landed on his stomach on the upper surface of the boulder. An unusually violent oscillation of the stone as a greater volume of water hit on its projecting fin pitched him off again, down beside us. He sat up, and I could see his lips moving as he swore. In light acrobatic kit it might have been easy to mount and cross the boulder, but we were all weighted by our guns and ammunition and equipment. A second jump landed him back on the quivering, bucking stone, and flat on his stomach he straightened himself so that his head pointed across the gorge. He straddled his legs, and, propelling himself by a series of jerks, grew dim and vanished in the mist.

Beside that magnificent exhibition of courage the man who first swallowed an oyster was a rank and sorry coward. I felt my teeth chattering with fright, and knew that if I stood there much longer with Bent the last shades of my resolution would vanish. So I leaped for the trembling bridge as Watkins had leaped, spread myself flat on the top of the boulder, and began to impel myself toward the far side as he had done.

It was a matter of a couple of inches or so of progress at each impulsion, and the total distance could not have been less than thirty feet. I had no idea of whether the next jerk would land me down in the invisible torrent under me, to meet a horrible death in the heated waters—I did not know whether Watkins had gone to the safety of the far bank or to extinction in the torrent. To the left of me was the vague white curtain of falling waters, beneath was the deafening thunder of the fall's impact, and as the varying volume of the cataract struck on the boulder's projecting fin it bucked and teetered under me until I prayed to encounter some knob or irregularity of surface that I might grip so as to lie still and recover my nerve. The top of the boulder was wet and smooth, and there was nothing for it but to go on; one jerk of the stone, such as had thrown Watkins off at his first attempt to get on, nearly slid me off into the unseen depths, but I wormed a way back to what I judged was the centre and wriggled my way along, not knowing whether I was following Watkins to death in the hot river or to the safety of its far bank.

In the middle, opposite where the falling water struck on the projecting fin of stone, the warm spray drenched me through and through, and I spared a thought from my fears to hope that my waterproof match-case was really so—it is odd how these little inconsequent thoughts come to relieve the mind in moments of stress. Out of the spatter of spray, I jerked my way along for a weary while, at intervals lying still to let the stone recover from an unusually heavy blow from the falling water. As in coming down the cliff, my paroxysm of fear spent itself, leaving only the mechanical action of the mind that kept my limbs at work to propel me across, and at long last I heard a welcoming yell, felt the grip of Watkins' hand as he eased my tumble to firm hold on the floor of the gorge beside him. While I lay there, recovering from the quivering nervous state to which the passage of the bridge had reduced me, Bent's white face came out of the reek and he dropped down beside me. I could still hear the sobbing of his breath as he lay on the rock, when such light as the mist permitted to reach us went out as if it had been turned off at a tap. There was no period of transition, but in a second we passed from mere gloom, in which we could distinguish each other's faces, to an impenetrable darkness, in which only the sense of touch, or the sound of our voices, could assure us of each other's presence.

My chief longing, there in the limit of darkness, was for something to smoke, I remember.

THE PLACE WHERE GHOSTS CHASE WOMEN

Holding on to each other, and guided by the roar of the cataract, we groped our way a few feet back from the brink of the river, and then sat touching each other to wait for light. It was like sitting blinded in a vapour bath; the heat from the river made a clammy moisture all about us, and we were soaked by the spray flung over the trembling bridge. I could feel moisture trickling down my face and under my clothes as I sat through the longest night it has ever been my luck to know.

We ate of our cooked meat, and from the time of the meal until dawn none of us spoke, as far as I can remember—the roar of the waters made speech a burden, and we were spent and weary with the descent of the cliff and the passage of that appalling bridge. I thought of a thousand things: of how we must clean our guns and pistols and put the cartridges and our matches in the sun to dry—if ever we saw the sun again; of old John Watkins—but he could not have been old when he came this way—dragging himself up the zig-zag path to die; of the paving of that wonderful road; of how John Watkins must have learned the language of the place, since in his mention of "the place where ghosts chase women" he had added—"so it is named." By whom?

I weighed in my mind whether Watkins or Bent had been right—was it right to venture on such a perilous path in ignorance of what its end would reveal? The answer to that was obvious—was it right for Columbus to sail from Palos toward the west? Why, after two years, was John Watkins glad to get away with no more than life—what had he or his Dutch companions done to render flight imperative, and why had "Nantia who rules monkeys" let them pass one way, and set her servitors on them when they returned? I wanted to put these unanswerable questions to Watkins to hear his conjectures, but thought that perhaps he slept.

The night was years long. I felt a sense of depression growing as it came toward dawn, as was only natural in the clammy, unhealthy heat. Only the wind blowing up toward the waterfall rendered the place bearable, and I judged that this wind was air sucked in toward where the volcanic heat, higher up the course of the river, made a vast boiler from which the stream emerged. That boiler was not always heated, though, for John Watkins' record told of how one of his companions had caught fish in this river. Again, in all probability the volume of the torrent was far from constant; if such a mass of water as fell now had been striking on the projecting fin for a century and a half, it would have worn that fin away; probably at times the stream was diminished to such an extent that the fall left the fin untouched—we had struck it at its worst, it seemed, for if the water had been cool enough for fish to live in it when John Watkins came he must have missed the added danger involved by the steamy mists.

I had given up hope of ever getting out from that devil's cauldron when, as suddenly as it had left us, the light came back. It showed the mist as thinner; fully half of the restless rock over which we had come was visible, and I could see the spray flung off from its projecting point. I could see, too, a distance that I judged to be about twenty feet up the face of the fall, but the top of the cataract was higher than that—I could not see the brink. It was a smooth, unbroken sheet of foamy white against which the eddying vapours beat as the wind drove up the gorge.

We got up weakly, for the night spent in such steamy heat was utterly enervating. We went back from the brink of the stream for about twenty yards and found ourselves against the wall of the chasm, turned to the right, and stumbled forward. It was in Watkins' mind to follow the wall of the cliff until he came to a path corresponding to the one by which we had come down; since the track on the opposite cliff had been made by human agency he concluded that there would be a corresponding path on this side.

As we went on the floor of the gorge grew more and more uneven; we had to climb over or work our way around boulders, step gingerly over clefts, and all the while search for the way upward. At last it showed, worn steps cut in the rock—what feet had worn down the edges of that stairway leading from danger to danger?

I counted as we went up, Watkins again leading, and

there were two hundred and ten steps, leading out on to a broad incline over which the cliff jutted—it was a road nine or ten feet in width, so that men might walk abreast for its full width under an arch of stone. This brought us to a reversing point similar to those of the opposite cliff. Here we came clear of the mist into such light as could reach down to us, and, looking upward, saw that the earth above was sunlit. No words can tell how good it was to see, even from these depths, sunlight falling on the world again.

We were sodden and, out from the warmth of the mist, shivering with cold. Our uncut hair hung lank and dead about our corpse-like faces, and the moisture dripped from our fortnight-old beards as the water ran out from our boots. We were past all telling exhausted, but Watkins plodded doggedly on, round the broad reverse where the road was cut double-width into the rock, and we two toiled on after him. A little way up from the reversing point the road narrowed until it was not more than the path on the opposite cliff, and Watkins took the lead and plodded upward. This wider portion, it seemed, had been the beginning of the greater work that the cutting of the narrow path foreshadowed, but those who hewed had been destroyed or driven away before the great task could be completed.

Since the preceding night we three had neither eaten nor drunk; we had filled our water-bottles at a pool on the floor of the gorge, first tasting the water to assure ourselves that it was drinkable, and finding it very slightly bitter, with a sulphury smell. For my part, I felt that the sight of the sodden cooked meat we carried would have sickened me. Watkins had a flask of concentrated meat lozenges as a sort of emergency ration, but since he did not judge this an occasion for using them it was not for me to suggest opening the flask.

We went on, and I was past fear, as I think was Bent. There came a time in that endless uphill trudge when I no longer cared whether I went on or fell; I grew angry with Watkins, angry with myself for being angry with him, and very angry indeed with Bent over his disinclination to cross the trembling bridge. It was a weak sort of petulance which sought some object on which to vent itself, and there was none.

The day grew older, and the sun came down to us. My feet ceased to leave wet marks on the rock pathway, and I could feel my clothes drying on me. At a little after noon we came to the last reversing point on the path, as I could see in turning. I could see, too, that the worst of the cliff journey was to come.

The angle of ascent was steeper—it was as if the people who cut this road had not quite settled in their minds, what was to be the angle and what width was necessary, when they began here—and the path narrowed to no more than a foot in width. We had to face toward the rock and struggle along with held breath, in the knowledge that one false step would send us down to lie pulped beneath the mists from which we had climbed. The difficulty of that last bit roused all the fight that was in me; I had not come thus far, and risked life on the trembling bridge, to fail at the last. My teeth were still clenched with the desperate effort of balancing on the awful ledge with which the path ended when I came out on the level and fell exhausted beside Watkins on the grass.

That grass was long and soft; from the edge of the cliff the ground sloped downward for a yard or two to form a little pocket, into which I rolled. There, without even troubling to loosen the rifle slung on my back, I slept, utterly exhausted, and so quickly that I did not see whether Bent came out from the gulf.

At about an hour from sunset Watkins shook me awake. He had spread out his share of the cooked meat on the rubbered side of his waterproof sheet, all but a chunk which he was eating. It was whitish, uninviting-looking stuff after its soaking in the waters of the chasm, but Watkins chewed determinedly.

"Better tuck into yours," he advised. "If you don't, it'll be crawling away from you before morning. I've had a look over there"—he jerked his thumb over his shoulder, in our direction of travel—"and there's no firewood and nothing to shoot, as far as I can see. We'll clean up our gear and sleep where we are, out of sight of prowlers. Get your meat out and tuck in."

He had already wakened Bent, who sat up, staring across the great chasm—I could see that he regretted his decision. Moving stiffly, I unpacked my meat ration

38

and forced down the greater part of it. I was aching in every joint, and, later, the movements necessary for cleaning my revolver and the rifle I carried proved actually painful, though doubtless they were good for me. Bent got through his share of the performance in sullen silence, and we let him sulk the fit out.

"Staying here," Watkins remarked as he rolled himself up in his waterproof sheet, "we are unsuspected by anyone on the track ahead—I put my head over the rise very carefully, but there was nothing in sight—it's a bare country. We'll have to get to game or starve to-morrow, but to-morrow can look after its own troubles."

With which bit of philosophy he curled himself up to sleep, it being just after sunset. I followed his example, as did Bent.

At dawn I was still stiff and obsessed with aches, but the rest had refreshened me, and I felt that all I needed was a wash and a shave—which were out of the question. Bent was awake, I saw, and sitting up; he looked less ill-tempered than on the preceding evening.

"Did you hear anything during the night?" he asked.

I shook my head. "Nothing short of Gabriel's trumpet could have made me hear," I said.

"I thought I heard something like bare feet on the grass, and a sort of clucking noise," he said. "I sat up and looked round, but there was nothing to see."

"And we're untouched," I remarked. "Well——" and I unrolled the corner of the waterproof in which I had packed the remains of my meat. But it was not well; it went over the edge of the cliff without a moment's delay. I heard Watkins chuckle.

"You might have been kinder, and given it a chance to walk down, Faulkner," he remarked.

"It might have turned on me," I said.

Our toilet consisted of yawning, stretching, and rubbing our eyes, and then, as there was nothing to eat, we had but to pack kit to be ready for the road. So, while the shadows yet lay long on the grass, and before the sun had soaked up all the dew, we topped the rise and looked out on the next stage of our journey.

The cliff edge, by the aneroid, was over five

thousand feet above sea level, and from before us the land fell away, entirely different in character from the country we had left on the far side of the gorge. It was hilly and broken, and we stood level with the tops of the highest hills; immediately in front of us a broad depression deepened gradually to form a valley between boundaries that were bare and sterile-looking, save for certain starved and stunted trees on the distant slopes. Away beyond the skyline the column of smoke that we had already seen appeared no nearer, and still there was a fold of ground between us and the crater that sent it forth. And there, running directly down the valley, was the trace of the great road.

"H'm!" Watkins remarked. "Don't see many restaurants open."

I thought of my meat that had gone over the cliff. Bent surveyed the uninviting prospect, and was dumb.

"There's a good fire over there," I said, nodding at the smoke from the distant volcano. "Perhaps we'll have something to cook by the time we get to it." I tried to emulate Watkins' light cheerfulness, and he gave me a smile for the poor attempt.

"Come on," he said. "It's a downhill road, and that means water. Water means grass, grass means game, game means food——"

We set out, following the trace of the buried road down the valley—even in this bare stretch it was buried under parched, arid soil, baked so hard that our boots left no marks. Save for a kite that sailed still-winged across the sky we saw no birds; on the ground were lizards and red woolly spiders here and there, and flies buzzed round our faces. There were no other signs of life. I wondered what the flies lived on, here, and whether the spiders and lizards lived on each other and so solved the problem of over-population of this waste land.

Up at the level of the chasm, and in the park-like stretch we had left, the air had been fresh and cool, but soon, as we went down the valley, it grew dryly hot—and we had but half a bottle of water apiece. Because of the thirst they would engender, Watkins reserved his meat-extract lozenges, intending that we should resort to them at nightfall if by then we found no alternative food. We dropped down and down from the cliff level as the day grew, and the hills on either side walled us in. At a little past noon we came to water, a trickle from under a rock to the left of the road that made green and weedy sward for about a hundred yards, before the earth that gave it took it back. With the point of the spear that I had stuck to even in crossing the trembling bridge I dug a hole in the ground, and we watched it fill, very slowly, from the spring, after we had finished the contents of our water-bottles. Watkins doled out two meat lozenges apiece; we had another drink, filled our water-bottles and travelled on, much refreshed.

The way was aridly monotonous. The valley continued, still sloping downward, and the hills on either side dropped their level consistently with that of the valley floor. The aneroid registered a descent of eighteen hundred feet from the level of the great chasm's top when we determined on camping for the night, having seen nothing eatable and still seeing no indications of game of any kind.

The place where we proposed to camp was a sort of widening of the valley down which the trace of the great road ran, and beyond it the valley narrowed as the hills on either side came so close to each other as to form a pass or defile. We were thus in a natural amphitheatre, in which were a score or more of great flat-topped boulders that looked as if giants had been throwing stones at each other. I suggested that we camp down under one of these.

"Better still, on one," Watkins amended. "It'll be no harder than the ground, and just in case visitors want to leave cards on us, we shall hear them coming up the garden path to the front door."

We had one more lozenge apiece, and a sparing drink to wash it down. Then we climbed, not easily, to the flat top of one of the great boulders, which would have slept a dozen of us and given room to spare. I lay awake for a long time wondering over the possibility of finding food on the morrow, but dozed off just as a radiance in the sky betokened the coming of the moon. It seemed but a second before the clutch of Bent's hand on my shoulder wakened me, but, opening my eyes, I saw the half of the waning moon well above the hills.

41

"Listen!" Bent hissed in my ear. "Can you hear it?"

I heard quite clearly a sound as if at a distance liquid were clucking out from a bottle—I can liken the noise to nothing else. It seemed to come from the direction of the buried road at first, and then from the direction in which we were travelling. Watkins, on the other side of me, drew his rifle toward him and clicked a cartridge from the magazine to the barrel chamber as quietly as possible. Then he lifted his head cautiously, and after a minute sat up. At that I, too, sat up, rifle in hand, and Bent took two cartridges from his pocket and loaded our shot-gun.

"What is it?" I whispered to Watkins, for the clucking, guggling sound seemed to be increasing in volume.

"Wait," he whispered back. "I can see nothing as yet. It's nothing dangerous, probably, or it would come more quietly. I rather think we're going to see something out of the ordinary."

I think I was first to see it, or rather them. From out the shadows under the hills to the right of the road something emerged into the light of the moon, something bulky and vague. At the same time, from where the hills converged to form a defile, came other shapes. They came with such grotesque antics that at first I took them for some large breed of monkey, but as they neared where we sat I saw that they were taller than any monkey stands and they kept upright. Yet—how shall I put it?—I had a feeling that they were not men.

My hair bristled with sudden terror—bear in mind that all three of us had been subjected to a limit of strain in the past two days, and were faint from want of food—and I heard Watkins suck in his breath with a sort of hiss; he too was moved beyond the ordinary, though he knew more than I did of the nature of these things. They came toward us without sound of footsteps, and yet they leaped and ran and sometimes spun round each other like dead leaves. There were scores of them, the maddest, most fantastic crew that ever troubled a nightmare.

They ran round in dizzy circles, they advanced and retreated in twos and threes, ever nearing the boulder on which we sat rigid and unbelieving. They were manlike in shape, but no men ever made humanity ludicrous as did these capering, guggling travesties; in the distance they had been impressive, but as they advanced into the open they became fearsomely absurd, hateful, and yet terrifying—it was as if they personified all the evil there is in the world, so that with them there came a sense of something demoniacal, polluting, utterly vicious. And as one leaping demon came within a score yards of us I nearly cried out; the moonlight showed him as indistinct in outline—there were no sharp contours against the light, but his edges were fuzzy, as if he were vignetted, or as if all round him the moon shone through thin fur.

In that particular, that ghostliness, haziness, as many as came near us were alike. I say as many as came near, for after the first score or so came others, scampering, clucking, devilish—the amphitheatre in the hills was alive with them, but it was a form of life that was most emphatically not human; it was inhuman in its capering glee, and we felt the presence of these things as that of something less than natural rather than supernatural. I felt myself bound from moving, as one is helpless in a dream, and fascinated, almost hypnotised, by the unceasing, whirling movements of these hazy shapes——

Crash! A charge of shot missed me by a miracle—Bent's trembling hand had inadvertently found the trigger of the loaded shot-gun that he held. At the flash and explosion the demons of the plain showed that they, too, knew what fear was. They ran faster than any man could run—they did not vanish, as would have vanished mere apparitions, but ran back into the shadows whence they had come, and in a couple of minutes the plain was empty.

"Was it—was it real?" I asked Watkins.

"I wouldn't believe what I read in that old diary," he answered slowly, "but it was true after all. And the writing in the cave—'the place where ghosts chase women'—this valley is that place."

He leaned over and tapped Bent on the shoulder.

"Better put that gun down," he said. "You won't hit the ghosts, but it seems as if you might hit us."

"What are they, Watkins?" I asked again.

He pulled his waterproof sheet about him as he sat,

and his sober, matter-of-fact air went far toward convincing me of my own sanity. "It's a long story, rather," he said, "and if I hadn't utterly disbelieved it I'd have told you before."

"It will pass the time if you tell me now—this is no place for sleep," I answered.

"It goes a long way back," he said, "out of historical times. You know the legend of Atlantis, the continent which is supposed to lie under the sea west of Africa?"

I nodded. "It's in Plato," Bent remarked.

"Exactly," Watkins agreed. "Well, Atlantis existed thousands of years ago, with men on it like you and me. But before that—thousands of years before, probably—there was another continent where the Pacific rolls to-day—all these islands are its mountain tops and tablelands. There was no life as we know it—the world was new and just shaping itself, then."

"And these—these things—are survivals?" I questioned.

He did not answer the question directly. "On that first continent," he said, "there were reptiles and low animal forms of life, but man did not evolve out of them as Darwin and his school of thought claimed. Man is a spirit—man came to earth as a spirit——"

"But——" I interrupted, remembering the unspiritual way in which these things had bolted. Watkins held up his hand.

"Wait," he bade. "Imagine the soul of a baby in the body of a grown man, without the experience of earthly life that we call intellect. Imagine further that the grown body containing that baby soul is—what we have just seen—not solid, material stuff like ourselves, but something that tries to make itself material, just as the baby tries to make itself an intellect from the moment its eyes are opened. These things have been trying for countless centuries to make themselves material, and they have accreted to themselves a certain amount of solidity—they had to run—they couldn't vanish ghost-fashion. But—to go back—man came to earth an untaught spirit, only half of what we are to-day, a hazy, far from material shape—less tangible than these things, by a long way. They were solid enough to make noises we could hear, they were curious, about us as monkeys or small children might be curious, afraid of us as small children might be afraid, which is why they came nearer only by degrees. And they were absolutely terrified by that gunshot noise."

"Half material," I said, "and not quite solid—I'm afraid I don't understand."

"Astral," Watkins said—a word that had no meaning for me. "Survivals from Lemuria, as that first continent of all was called. You remember the Neanderthal man, and the Piltdown skull?"

I nodded. "I've heard of them," I said.

"Well, if you ever get a chance to look at the reconstructed Piltdown type, you'll see that it's virtually animal, and not man at all. It was the highest type of its day in the animal world, but still it was mere animal, nothing more. When man came to earth as a spirit, he made himself one with the Piltdown animal type, and from the blending of animal instinct and the spirituality that came to make man resulted intellect—you get in all the human race to-day a perpetual warring of the spirit against the flesh, the higher sense trying to conquer the lower instincts. That is typical of the blending—the amalgamation of the two parts of man, untaught soul and animal instinct, which together make for intellectual progression. The Piltdown type had the animal instinct, and grafting on to that the spirit produced thought, memory, intellect—the development of the soul. And the Lemurian ghost, as you may call it, had just as much need of the Piltdown brute as that had of the spirit, to produce man as he is now."

"But these things—they could never produce normal men, no matter what they were blended with," I said. "They were evil, essentially evil—I could feel it when they came near."

"Precisely," Watkins said. "When man in the mass came to earth as spirit, there was some portion of the spirit group that was too essentially evil to blend even with the Piltdown type—it remained, striving after but never accomplishing material shape. That is what we have seen, the dregs left from human forming, evil essences, powerless against us, but able to make us feel their hatefulness by their mere presence."

45

I was still unconvinced. "How is the grafting done, as you call it—how can such things amalgamate, as you say?" I asked.

"Probably they'll tell us that at Kir-Asa," he answered. "Anyhow, think it over—it's a more reasonable theory of evolution than Darwin's. There's no missing link, in this chain, between the instinct of the animal and the intellect and reasoning power of man."

He lay down again and left me wondering. Once or twice I thought I saw capering forms in the shadows, but it is easy to imagine in an uncertain light, and it may have been fancy. Then came dawn.

We sat up, hungry, and looked toward the defile. Of our visitors of the night no sign remained. The curving defile through which the trace of the road led ended our perspective, the natural amphitheatre in which we sat on the boulder was bare and arid as had been all the journey from the chasm. There was nothing for it but to go on, and to take what fate might have in keeping for us beyond the pass in the hills.

THE WOMAN WHO RULED MONKEYS

We came on her just after passing the narrow neck or defile that shut in the valley at its eastern end. She sat on a low rock beside the trace of the ancient road, the first human being we had seen since we passed through the gorge—except for the three head-hunters she was the first since we dragged our boat up out of reach of the tides. One great ape, squatting quietly beside her, peered at us and then went on searching his stomach for lice; another lay beside the boulder, stretched out with its head on its forearm, too lazy even to look up at us.

It was a sudden encounter, for a point of the hill on the right of our way jutted out, and she sat just beyond the point; for her there could have been nothing unexpected about our coming, for Bent and I were talking about the things we had seen in the night, and there was the noise of our footsteps, too. Probably she had waited here with her monkey guard since the report of the shot-gun warned her of strangers coming down the valley.

She was tall and well-formed—she stood up as we approached—and clothed in a robe of coarse, dirty-grey linen, held in at the waist by a belt that looked like plaited strips of the same material. I have seen Spanish women with darker skins; the cast of her features was good, even fine, and the black hair, long and tied back at the nape of her neck, was not lank and dead looking as is that of many eastern women, but rather wavy, and glossy-looking, as if it were well-kept. I describe her thus particularly because she was typical of the women we were to see here, as a race, although there were exceptions, of course.

Her age I judged as somewhere round the late thirties or early forties. Her face was finely moulded, but spoilt by a habitually angry expression, though as she rose, staring at Watkins, there was a questioning, puzzled look in her eyes for a few seconds. She spoke in a commanding voice, evidently giving us an order, and stretched out her hand toward the valley, pointing us back the way we had come.

"Madam, I disagree," Watkins said blandly. "We have not done a tight-rope performance in front of a young Niagara to be pushed back by your music-hall turn. We are going on."

She stood pointing, statuesque. The sleepy brute beside its scratching mate sat up and yawned—I think they were orang-outang in breed, but am not certain; they were great, dangerous-looking brutes, I know.

"Rifles loose," Watkins said—he already had his own ready—"and back to back triangle fashion if trouble begins." He took a step forward. I got my rifle ready, and Bent loaded the shot-gun.

The woman also took a step forward, and almost shrieked a command as she gestured us to return up the valley. Watkins patted his stomach and pointed to his open mouth. "If you'd kindly lead us to a quick lunch-bar, or even a coffee-stall——" he suggested.

Then this strange being facing us—she stood directly in our way now—let loose a torrent of angry language, and as it flowed I saw Watkin's expression change; he listened intently, even frowning with the effort at comprehension. The woman's harangue wound up with a verbal firework discharge, a sort of effort at condensing the arguments into ten seconds of throaty assault and battery.

Our position was a deadlock. If we moved another couple of steps, we should have to push this woman out of our way, and to touch her would in all probability result in bringing her monkeys on us. As she stood silent, expecting us to obey her obvious behest and go back the way we had come, Watkins expressed our intention in his own inimitable way.

"I'd hate to get your monkey up over this, madam," he said, "but we—are—going—on."

She spoke a dozen syllables in reply, slowly and distinctly, and then Watkins amazed me. Carefully and with obvious effort, he answered her in her own language, or in an equivalent near enough for her to understand. I knew, then, why he had tried so hard to catch words of her former rapid harangue.

The effect was electrical. She sprang back and called a guttural command. The two great brutes by the boulder looked up, saw her finger pointed at us, and leaped to obey—we had barely time to form our triangle, so quickly did the situation change. One of the beasts, springing at me, got the muzzle of my rifle between his teeth as his paws clutched the barrel, and I pulled the trigger, blowing the back of his skull out. Watkins dropped the other in mid-charge, and we moved forward.

But the woman leaped on her boulder and screamed aloud in a frenzy of rage. Then down the slopes behind her, from unsuspected crannies in the rocks and from concealment behind scrubby bushes, came the main body of her guard, great brutes that tumbled and clawed their way down in answer to her call.

I heard Watkins whistle his dismay before he picked off the foremost of the herd, and saw the woman's face express fear. Evidently the killing at close quarters ranked as a normal business in her mind, but this ability to kill at a distance was a different matter, and she saw doubt as to the outcome of the fight.

But I had little time to observe her. Aiming carefully, I accounted for two of the monkeys at about thirty yards range, and Watkins bagged two more. Bent could do no effective work with the shot-gun, so far, for the brutes were beyond its range; besides, the triangular defence we made gave him the rear to watch, though he was able to keep an eye on what we were doing as well. He could only wait, helplessly, and the strain of waiting accounted for what followed.

We had seven of our assailants dead, and three more were howling and kicking on the ground, disabled. The others hesitated, for there is enough glimpse of reason in these brutes to give them glimmerings of fear, and they connected up the noise of the rifle shots with the deaths of their companions—and they were acting by order of the woman, not because their blood was warmed by close encounter. But, at their hesitation, the woman danced with rage on the boulder, and shrieked a torrent of commands at them; it was evident that she had them as thoroughly under control as a huntsman with a well-trained pack of hounds, for the foremost dozen or more of the beasts bunched themselves for a charge.

Watkins yelled to the woman to call them off, and she shrieked back that we should die where we stood—he told me the purport of that interchange afterward.

"Aim well, Faulkner," he said to me. "Our lives hang on it."

I had recharged my magazine. The woman cried out again and they came at us. Then Bent, who could understand the whole business perfectly, but, having no rifle, could do nothing against the monkeys, lost his nerve as the chattering herd of bestiality began its charge. He swung round and, lifting his shot-gun, fired at the woman on the boulder at little more than ten yards' range.

Her commanding cries gave place to a scream of pain and terror; she flung up her arms, and with blood pouring from her mouth—Bent's shot had taken her full in the breast—pitched headlong from the boulder to the ground and died. Her monkeys, hearing her scream, and galled by the fire of the two rifles, pulled up as her voice ceased to urge them, and then turned and fled back to the shelter of the hill. I drew a long breath of relief; it was the ugliest form of death I had ever faced.

The monkeys gave no sign of coming to resume the attack. Freed from the urge of their mistress' voice, they feared the roar from the rifles' throats and the leaping fire that struck them from a distance. I had a feeling that the last barrier was passed.

There were four of the brutes, so wounded by our expanding bullets that they could not drag themselves away; to these we put an end with our revolvers, and the herd was eighteen short of its strength at the beginning of the fight. It was short of a mistress, too, and we were unscratched, though, as our original total of ammunition was two hundred rounds per rifle, we could not afford many fights like this.

And Bent—somehow that shot of his changed the way in which I regarded him, while Watkins felt a change too. All the way he had been with us, but not of us, a protesting member, and now he had saved our lives—but by shooting a woman.

She was a fiendish sort of woman who would have laid on her beasts till they overcame our fire and tore our limbs apart. It was, in the long run, her life or ours, unless we had kept the monkeys off until they sickened from the attack—an unlikely chance, from what we saw of her marvellous control of the herd, and the change in their demeanour after her fall. Bent had saved our lives—but he had shot a woman.

It was not for us to pass judgment on what he had done, and we knew it. To assess that shooting, one must have stood as Bent stood, with nerves shaken by the passage of the trembling bridge and by our encounter of the preceding night, half-starved, waiting with a useless weapon—useless against such things as these, at least—for the chances of our two rifles beating off the attack—or failing. We knew full well that we had no right to judge him, nor did we openly question what he had done, and yet from that point onward there was a difference in our relations. Hitherto he had been a protesting companion, whom we had tried to make see as we saw; we both tried to retain that level of intercourse, but the very effort made a widening of the gulf between him and ourselves, and I know he felt the change.

I wonder still over this, regret it still; we could not help the feeling, and did our best to conceal it, but I wonder if we were sufficiently mindful of the fact that one of us might have been driven to do what he did—though it had not occurred to us as a solution of our difficulty—and if the existence of a change of attitude toward him stamped us as sentimental ingrates. Well, there it was, an unpleasant feeling to be put out of our thoughts. Outwardly, we neither praised nor blamed, but turned our minds to the business of getting on our way.

"But first," Watkins said, " we must bury the woman—we can't go on and leave the corpse lying here. There's food near by for us—she must have had something to live on."

We made a grave under the hillside and covered in the body with earth and rocks, and it will simplify matters to state now that we could not have been clear of the place many hours before those infernal monkeys grubbed out the earth and pulled their mistress' corpse to light again. When our self-imposed task was done, Watkins mopped his brow wearily.

"I've had enough in the last three days to last me a year," he announced. "I'm tired, mortally tired of excitements, and want a rest and a bath and a shave and a hair cut and a good square meal. We'll move on and look for them."

In due course we found them all, though not in the order in which he placed them. To begin with, a half-mile or so further on we came to two great rocks that leaned against each other, forming a shelter in the shape of an inverted V. The back of this shelter was roughly thatched with reeds on transverse poles, and the front was closed by a reed and pole door which lifted bodily aside to give entrance—it stood beside the open entry when we saw the place. Within was a dirty-looking bed on the ground, made up of skins and such coarse linen as the monkey woman had worn; there were sundry other rough fitments, and, what interested us most, a sort of wicker basket containing a dozen eggs—duck eggs, rather small—a big stone jar of water, another jar of maize meal, and a bunch of about twenty ripe plantains.

"Move along and get some wood for a fire," Watkins said to me. "Mine is boiled duck eggs."

I hastened to obey; there was scrubby stuff on the hillside which seemed placed specially for our use, and in ten minutes the eggs were in our cooking pot and on the fire. We made a sort of thick porridge with the meal; eggs, in spite of the absence of salt, and the porridge vanished like a dream, and the plantains followed. We sat, full and content and drowsy.

"That monkey keeping must be a sort of permanent job," Watkins remarked. "Apparently it's a defence of the defile here. It's just as well, for our own sakes, that we buried the woman—we might get into trouble with the inhabitants here if they found we had killed her in addition to smashing up the monkeys—for which they could hardly blame us."

"What is the language she used?" I asked.

"The nearest I can tell you, so far, is that it's a sort of bastard Persian," he answered. "It's a dialect built on a Sanskrit foundation—in my youth I studied Sanskrit, for it's the key to every Aryan language or dialect in the East, and I always meant to come East. I must stuff you two."

"Stuff us?" Bent asked.

"Fill you up with words that will be useful—it's astonishing what you can do in a language if you know three or four hundred words in common use. If you hear it and have to make yourself understood in it, the construction of sentences very soon comes to you. That is, if the language is built on an Aryan foundation, as this is."

He began the stuffing process that day, and I remember that the first lesson consisted of equivalents for such every-day words as "yes," "no," "give," "I have," "have you," "we are," "maize," "eggs," "water," and other commonplaces. But that came later.

We moved on within an hour of our meal. The valley ended at the top of an escarpment from which we surveyed a great plain, so broad that the hills which ringed it in were blue hazed in the far distance. Far away before us rose the squat cone of the volcano whose smoke-column we had seen from beyond the great chasm, and stretching away from beneath our feet toward the volcano was an ordered, fertile land of which every yard appeared to be under cultivation. Beside the sheen of rivers or canals thatched huts showed, and here and there, as far as details of the land were distinct enough for us to see, was a grey stone edifice with its thatched huts round it. Away toward the volcano I could see a grey indistinctness rising out the cultivated lands, and toward it Watkins stretched a pointing hand.

"Kir-Asa at last," he said.

We had no field-glasses, so could not verify his conjecture. Nearer, however, was something with which we were more immediately concerned, for at the foot of the escarpment on which we stood was a line of water—evidently an irrigating canal, for it ceased where the trace of the road met it at right angles. A little way beyond the canal the road had apparently been uncovered, for in place of the mere trace on which we stood was a clearly-defined, smooth, grey highway which went across the plain toward the distant volcano.

There were figures working in the cultivated area beyond the irrigating canal, but none within a mile or more of where we stood. So far we were unobserved, for all that we could see. We conjectured that the hills had shut in the noise of our fight with the monkeys, or else this was an incurious race.

"That water looks peculiarly inviting," Watkins said, and we set off down the slope without further delay.

I had got my pack off, preparatory to stripping for a bath, when Watkins sprang a surprise on us. He produced a neat little flannel package, secured from damp by being enclosed in an oiled silk bag, and, unrolling it, exhibited a carefully greased pair of nail scissors, a safety razor and packet of blades, and two nickelled cylinders of which one proved to be a shaving brush and the other a stick of real shaving soap—luxuries of which I had not dreamed on such a trip as this.

We cut each other's hair—I had an easy time barbering Watkins, for it simply amounted to trimming the fringe that grew round the patch where, as he put it, experience had rubbed the fur off. Then he cut my thick crop, and cut it badly; by that time Bent had finished shaving. I cut his hair while Watkins shaved, and then it was my turn with the razor. After that, stripped and in the water, I scrubbed myself with mud from the bank and with the nail brush which formed my own contribution to our toilet set.

53

I set down these little details because they were not little to us then. After our experiences of the past fortnight, they were simply wonderful luxuries, as was that of sitting stark naked on the bank while our shirts and socks, which we had scrubbed with mud for soap, dried in the sun. We carried spare shirts and socks, of course, but all were dirty—this was the first big clean-up in which we had been able to indulge since leaving the coast, and it was hard to realise that little more than a fortnight had elapsed since we dropped off the tramp steamer into our boat.

There was added luxury in the feeling that came of putting clean clothing on to our clean skins. We sat facing toward the canal and gazing at the fertile land beyond—little of it was visible from this lower level, for the cultivated areas were interspersed with patches of woodland where the reed huts were placed.

"I'd give one ear for a good smoke," Watkins said lazily.

"It can't be done," I told him, "and since one good meal doesn't last all day, what about looking for the duck that laid those eggs?"

"Any old duck," he agreed, "I shan't stop to examine the vintage. But by the look of things we're out of the wilds, back among a sort of people that it will be best not to offend—we don't want to be taken prisoners at the outset, like my brave old ancestor and his band. I decree that we keep friendly with whoever turns up, unless we're forced to make a fight for it, and since nobody seems to have witnessed our shooting among the monkeys, we don't pull a trigger except to save life in the last extremity. In all probability the inhabitants here don't know what a firearm is, and as long as we don't shoot we shall have a deadly surprise up our sleeves for use at need. Do you agree?"

"Most emphatically, as long as we can get food without shooting," I said.

"John Watkins got back with his powder all spent, according to the inscription in the cave," Bent suggested.

"There would be no real memory of what a shot is like, after this lapse of time, though there might be a tradition," Watkins answered. "That is, unless these people know the use of gunpowder, which is not

54

likely."

"I agree, anyhow," Bent said, "as long as we can pull through without shooting."

"Then that's settled," Watkins remarked in a satisfied way. "Now I suggest we pack up and get along, behave like perfect little gentlemen when we meet the natives, and try and manoeuvre that duck—roast, with sage and onion stuffing, for choice."

He sat gazing across the plain, reluctant to stir himself in spite of his suggestion; the smoke from the volcano, whose crater we could no longer see at this level, went up in an unbroken column until it thinned and broke in the upper air. Suddenly Watkins slapped his leg.

"Got it!" he exclaimed.

"What?" I asked. "A mosquito?"

"I've been wondering, ever since I read the inscription why Kir-Asa was written like that, 'Asa' under 'Kir.' That's what it must be—Asa the city under Kir the mountain, and he wrote it that way when he had learned something of the language. It was hyphened in Philip Watkins' diary, but this is why the inscription put one half under the other."

And, as usual, he was right.

NER-AG

By noon, when we were beginning to feel the need of that roast duck, we came on a man hoeing in a field of young maize. He was naked down to the waist, whence depended a sort of petticoat that ended at his knees; he wore leg wrappings of coarse grey linen, rolled puttee-fashion, and—sure sign of some degree of civilisation—boots, the hair of the hide still on the leather. We came on him quietly, and the noise he made at his work prevented him from hearing us, while the fact that his back was turned our way accounted for his not seeing, until Watkins spoke to him and turned him round.

"Ho!" Watkins said—he was careful to observe later that the pun on the man's occupation was unintentional. And here I would remark that I have set down the general tenor of his conversations with these people as he explained them to me until I gained enough mastery of the language—which was very soon—to understand fully what was said.

The worker turned and looked at us in a scared way. He was the male complement of the woman who had ruled monkeys, in racial characteristics, though darker skinned, and without her angry expression. He straightened himself, looked at Bent and at me, and gazed hard at Watkins. Then he dropped on one knee on the ground and bowed his head, evidently with the deepest respect.

"H'm!" Watkins remarked thoughtfully, "apparently I'm better looking than I thought." Then, to the man, in the equivalent language the woman of the monkeys had spoken: "We need food and rest—lead us to them."

Without a moment's hesitation the man shouldered his hoe and came toward us. "Lord, I obey," he said simply, as if it were the most natural thing on earth that strangers should suddenly appear and demand his services.

He led the way to the road; here it fulfilled the promise of the trace we had followed, for it was no longer buried under the accretions of the ages. Full sixty-feet in width it ran, a smooth pavement of squared rock, and we learned later, where a portion of the edge had been broken away, that the blocks of stone so wonderfully fitted to each other were a good eighteen inches in thickness, set in a bituminous kind of cement that made a foundation as hard and enduring as rock itself. Except that an earthquake might shatter it, such a road would endure for ever, and in spite of everything I am still inclined to count it the greatest wonder of Kir-Asa.

Along this magnificent highway our guide conducted us for more than a mile; then he turned off to the right, led us up a short avenue bordered by palms and plantains and flowering shrubs, coming at last to the front of a one-storied building of grey stone, with curtains of woven cane hanging in its unglazed window spaces, and a door of reed thatched on to cane to close the entrance. This door simply lifted aside, bodily, and when in its place its cross-bars fitted into slots in the stone wall. Odd though it may seem, nobody among this race had ever thought of swinging doors on hinges, or else they were not enterprising enough to translate thought into action.

Three other men, dressed similarly to the one we had followed, were doing nothing by the entrance as we approached. They made obeisance to Watkins as our guide had done, a thing which puzzled me, since they were not even interested in Bent or myself. At a sentence from our man, one of these three men ran within the house and presently returned with a superior personage, who wore a tunic above the kilt or petticoat of the labourers, and in addition had a leather belt to which was attached a sheathed knife with a carved wooden handle. His superiority was still further proved by the fact that his clothes were spotlessly clean.

He, too, did deep reverence to Watkins, and evidently waited that person's will.

"We need food and rest," Watkins condescended to explain again, and let the simple statement show that he intended to live up to the position accorded him. I had not the faintest idea why the mere sight of him set these people bowing and scraping.

"Lord, come," the new, clean man invited him. We followed, all three, down a long, dim corridor; our escort lifted a door at the end and leaned it against the wall, motioning us to pass through the doorway.

We entered a spacious, well-lighted room, and, looking upward, I saw the reedy thatch of the building on bamboo rafters. From a skin-covered couch at the far side of the room a man rose at our entrance, and as I saw his face I understood why Watkins had been greeted with so much respect. For in spite of different clothing, greater height, and darker skin, the man who faced him might have been his twin brother, so closely did they resemble each other.

A sentence from the inscription in the cave flashed back into my mind—"this year, being freed, we fledd and returned——" John Watkins, in the two years he spent here, had made a closer relationship than we had guessed.

For once our Watkins lost his habitual self-possession. "And who the devil may you be?" he asked, in good nervous English.

57

The man facing us was equally startled. "Speak!" he commanded, of course in his own tongue. "Whence came you?"

"From the chasm beyond the hills—from the sea beyond the chasm," Watkins answered him, speaking slowly in the man's own language. Or rather, he spoke in a language so nearly like it as to be understood. There were naturally differences between the equivalent he knew and the language of this people whom he had never seen before.

"Who are you, with my face?" the man asked again.

Watkins smiled. "Who are you, with my face?" he echoed.

The man drew himself up proudly. "I am Ag, son of Ner, called Ner-Ag," he announced. "Here I rule under the king the lands of the west, with power of life and death. Who are you?"

"Say, Ag son of Ner," Watkins said, choosing his words carefully, "is there not in the records of your fathers a tale of a strange man from the west?"

Ag, son of Ner, permitted himself to smile faintly. "It is no tale, but truth, there was such a one," he answered. "One who came with others from the west, and fled back to the west."

"He was of my house. I am Philip, son of Wat Kins (he separated the name into two words) and blood kin to you, Ag, son of Ner."

If either had doubted the claim, he had but to look at the other's face to find proof.

"And these?" Ag asked, looking first at Bent and then at me.

"This"—Watkins indicated me first—"is Jack, son of Faulk, and this"—gesturing at Bent—"is Cecil, son of Bent. We need food, and rest, man of my blood and breed, having passed many dangers to come to you."

"How came you past the guard of beasts in the pass?" Ag inquired.

"We overcame them by our magic, and so came unharmed, as you see," Watkins answered readily.

"Strong magic," said Ag. He appeared to reflect for a minute, then: "Come," he bade, and himself led us to another large room, half-way along the corridor through which we had been conducted to him. On the way he issued an order to the cleanly-robed

58

major-domo who had escorted us before, and who still lingered in the corridor.

In this second room was a table, a solid block of grey rock, recessed for knee room, and furnished with backless, fur-covered settees like that on which Ag had been seated. Presently there appeared servants, naked down to the waist as had been the labourers in the fields, carrying wooden platters of food, a stone jug of water, wooden—or rather sectioned and thinned bamboo—drinking vessels without handles, and knives, but no forks. When I had time to examine one of the knives I found its metal identical with that of the spear I had brought with me.

Watkins looked at me with a broad smile, and nodded at the dishes on the table. Among them was one in which, very obviously, were two cold roast ducks. There was a crumbly sort of bread or cake made principally from maize flour, and there were some sweet concoctions in which plantain and maize flour cooked together figured—I found later that it was the custom of these people to begin on their sweet dishes, a habit to which I never grew partial.

"Kinsman and guest," said Ag, "eat your fill, you and Jack and Ce Cil"—he stumbled over the name—"and when you have eaten and rested, we will talk of your coming here."

He must have been burning with curiosity about us, as indeed we were about him and his surroundings. Yet he sat by us with scarcely a remark while we ate, and then conducted us to a third room, in which were slightly larger settees, with hard pillows which converted them into beds.

"Rest," said Ag, "and at sunset we will eat together, Philip son of Wat Kins, blood kin to me."

With that he left us. We unslung our rifles, got rid of our packs—we had stuck closely to all our gear, so far, the limit of relaxation consisting in carrying our hats instead of keeping them on our heads—and sat down on the settees, retaining only revolvers and ammunition belts by way of precaution.

"Well?" Bent asked, looking at Watkins.

"A right noble man, this kinsman of mine," Watkins answered, "and one after my own heart. The stars in their courses fight for us, and the luck is too good to last. Roast duck, as ordered, but they overlooked the sage and onion stuffing."

With which mixture of grave reflection and his usual quaint comment on unusual circumstance, he lay down and composed himself to sleep as peacefully as if he had lived here for years. Strange though it may seem, in five minutes I too was sound asleep. We had passed through so much in so little time, and had had so little respite from anxiety and strenuous work, that I was quite content to let the future solve its own problems, and to take the offered rest.

We were awake before sunset and had just decided that we could safely leave our packs and rifles, if we held on to the revolvers, when Ag entered the room.

We rose, and stood waiting, but with a smile he motioned us to sit again, and himself sat down on one of the settees, beside Watkins. He touched the revolver holster on the ammunition belt Watkins had put on in accordance with our decision.

"I would question," he said, "concerning some few things. What is this you wear?"

"It is a strong magic that brings sleep," Watkins answered, unhesitatingly and truthfully; the belt held fifty revolver cartridges.

"What purpose brought you to this land?" Ag asked next.

"A tale that your ancestor told before he died," Watkins answered with equal readiness. "For, Ag my kinsman, there is in some men a hunger that drives them forth from the quiet of a home and the sound of a woman's voice, a restlessness that bids them set foot in perilous places for the quest of things new over which to wonder. So do I know hunger—so do I quest."

Ag looked squarely at him. "Philip, man of my blood, have you come to this land in the desire of power, or in peace?"

"In peace, Ag," Watkins said, returning the steady gaze.

Ag looked away, satisfied. Probably he would have questioned further, but the tinkling of a distant bell interrupted him. He led us to the room in which we had eaten before, and in which, apart from eight servants ranged stiffly round the walls to execute any wish that Ag or his people might express, three persons waited our coming.

There was a woman, darker of skin than any I had yet seen, whom Ag introduced formally to Watkins and through him to us as Niala, his wife; there was a girl—woman, perhaps—of twenty-three, Ag's daughter Eve, and a boy of about fifteen, Ner, his son. In all families of rank, we found the eldest son took the name of his grandfather; this boy, for instance, would be known as Ag-Ner when he came to man's estate, and his son again would be known as Ner-Ag, and commonly called Ag. The custom saved trouble in finding names, I thought. As to the girl's name, I wondered if, like Ag's resemblance to our Watkins it was another legacy left by old John; regarding that we could get no evidence either way, except that we found no other instance of the use of the name.

The boy was dark, and had his mother's cast of face; the girl, on the other hand, was light. The son, who reproduced his mother's characteristics, was very obviously her favourite child. I gathered that, as is often the case, Ag had more affection for his daughter than for his son.

Eve's wavy, dark brown hair—it was not quite black—was tied in at the nape of her neck, and thence fell half-way to her hips. Both she and her mother wore plainly cut robes of white linen, embroidered above the belt that defined the waist line, and thence falling in graceful folds to the ankle; their dainty shoes were made from thin strips of leather plaited so as to form patterns—I have seen similar work on hunting crop handles; for ornament they wore necklaces of what I took to be little green glass beads, but later we found that these were pierced and threaded emeralds, cut without facets and polished smooth. The art of making glass had been lost among these people, though specimens of glass work, highly prized, still survived in the country.

Ag and his son wore the low-necked tunic, the kilt to the knee, and the leg wrappings and boots normal with males of the country, though in their cases the finest of linen and the softest of leather served as material. I set down these details as necessary, though perhaps tedious.

61

We ate, a friendly party, though Bent and I were handicapped by the fact that Watkins had given us only one ration of his "stuffing." I caught a word here and there, and Eve, seated next to me, added to my knowledge of the language by pointing out such common things as knife, salt, or the floor, and getting me to repeat the name. My difficulties over pronunciation made it a merry lesson.

She had, in addition to a grace that was her own, the dignity that made her father a man we already respected and liked, and with these—or perhaps in spite of them—a spirit of mischievous laughter that made her a charming personality. She had great, dark brown eyes, still pools of liquid light—she was beautiful even among this race of women, among whom scarcely one could be called unattractive, and hers was beauty of soul as well as of face and form. Already, with the barrier of language between us to a great extent, I felt her charm, and Bent, whom the boy and his mother tried to interest, marked our sudden friendship enviously, I thought.

Suddenly I saw that Watkins was telling Ag of our journey. He balanced a knife on its back between two wooden platters, and rocked it with his finger to illustrate the trembling bridge. Eve becoming absorbed in the description, as was the boy, included Watkins, myself and Bent in a general glance of admiration. We were all heroes to her from them onward.

But Watkins went on to tell of our journey down the valley, and when he used the phrase—"the place where ghosts chase women"—Ag put up a hand and stopped him.

"Kinsman Philip," said Ag, "you err in ignorance of the customs of our country. Before our women that place is never mentioned."

I saw that both Eve and her mother looked distressed, as if—as if indecent language had been used, to put it plainly. For some reason that we could not guess, the ghosts were as unmentionable as obstetrics in a mixed English company.

In an awkward silence Ag put some question into which the word "Nantia" came, and in turn Watkins questioned him. It was a hereditary title, we found, held for the time being by the woman in charge of the monkey guard which was set to prevent what they called "poison-dart people" from entering the country. I rejoiced to hear later from Watkins that the use of poisoned missiles had been prohibited among these people long ago, under pain of death, and the trick of making the poison, even, had practically died out. It was used for executions, and for nothing else; as crime and consequent execution were rare, there was little call for the poison, which was made only in Kir-Asa at need.

For the rest, the race was peaceful, mainly agricultural in its pursuits, and gradually decreasing in numbers owing to a very low birth rate. The country had no distinguishing name, since lack of intercourse with any other country rendered one unnecessary; it was about thirty miles by forty in extent, supporting something over two hundred thousand inhabitants. There was a king, but he had become insane about five years before, and authority was vested for the time in a council of five, among whom Ag had most power. At the king's death the eldest of his three sons, a man now nearly thirty years old, would rule, but by the custom of the country his authority could not be recognised in his father's lifetime—hence the rule of the council. There was but one city, Kir-Asa, of which one of the council of five was governor; Ag and the other three parcelled out the country between them as provincial rulers. These facts Watkins elicited that evening; we learned more later.

We sat long over the fragments of the meal. Eve and I got on famously, in spite of linguistic difficulties. I had a little oval pocket mirror, with silver frame and lid—which hinged backward to form a stand—and with bevelled glass, and toward the end of the evening I took it out to show her her own eyes, while we were trying to converse. She took it from me and examined it reverentially, almost; the hinged cover was a miracle to her, and the glass itself—I had no idea, then, of the value of glass among these people—was to her what a diamond necklace would be to a civilised woman. At last she held it out to me regretfully—I could see she coveted it.

I managed two words, thanks to Watkins' tuition. "I give," I said, making no move to take the mirror.

She looked at me, and blushed before her eyes drooped. Then she shook her head, and with a certain assumption of pride held the mirror out for me to take. But I smiled, repeating: "I give."

Still she refused the gift. I had a brilliant idea.

"Watkins," I said, in a pause in his converse with Ag, "tell this lady that this little present is my way of showing appreciation of her father's hospitality, and I won't take it back."

With a twinkle in his eyes, Watkins translated the desired message. After a pretty little pause of hesitation, Eve signified her pleased acceptance. Then she rose to show the trinket to her father and mother, who stared incredulously at the bevelled glass, and even her brother looked envious of her luck, though why they should make all this fuss over a mere pocket mirror was more than we could tell, then. The intrinsic value of the thing, by their standards, made it a notable gift, and I fancy I went up in Ag's estimation.

Well, it was a trivial incident in itself, but perhaps the way in which I recall it will show the power of Eve's brown eyes.

Only a few minutes later a scared looking servitor—it was the nice, clean man we had met at the entrance to the house—put his head in at the doorway and spoke something to Ag in which I caught the word "Nantia." Ag rose and went out instantly, and in the dead silence which ensued I caught Watkins' warning look at me. I saw his lips set tight in a way that I had come to know, and sensed trouble waiting for us, not far off.

KIR-ASA

I saw Eve glance from one to other of us three nervously, almost fearfully, as Ag went out and constraint fell on us who remained. So easily and naturally had we fitted into the ways of this friendly household—except for the mention of the ghosts—that we had practically forgotten the strangeness and possible dangers of our position when this reminder was suddenly thrust on us. I saw Watkins unobtrusively loosening his revolver in its holster, and followed his example. Then we waited, perforce.

At last Ag came back. He spoke a word of command and the eight servants who still stood by the walls went out. When he judged them quite out of hearing, Ag spoke.

"Philip, son of Wat Kins," he said gravely, "one of my people who went to the pass to take food to the Nantia has returned, bringing word that she and certain of the beasts lie dead."

"It was the price of resisting our advance through the pass," Watkins said coolly, resting a hand as if by accident on his revolver butt, and looking frankly up at his interlocutor.

"Peace!" Ag bade. "Make no confession that might force me to judge. I have already decided that I will not judge, else had I not spoken, and accused, before my wife and children. For in my hands, should I judge, is power of life and death."

"Not over us," Watkins contradicted quietly. "The magic by which we passed the beasts is more potent than any force used against us."

At the boldness of that speech Ag frowned, for never before had his power been called in question. But he put the personal feeling aside—a great man, was Ag.

"Philip, my kinsman," he said, "between us is the bond of race, and you with Jack son of Faulk and Ce Cil son of Bent have eaten with me and in my house—I will not judge. Yet not even I, Ner-Ag"—he used his full title to mark the gravity of his speech—"can prevent your trial and perhaps your sentence."

"And that is . . .?" Watkins asked.

"One of you killed the Nantia—for that one, death," Ag answered solemnly. "For the others, deprivation of all rights, since they were accessory."

Watkins, not yet familiar with the intricacies of the language, puzzled this out to his satisfaction. We two waited, uncomprehending, but understanding that danger had recurred for us in some form.

"As to rights, since we have none we can be deprived of none," Watkins said at last. "And we were driven to fight—it was kill or be killed."

Ag shook his head. "The Nantia is sacred—on her the safety of the pass depends, and failing her presence the poison-dart people would come in and destroy us.

65

Who attempts to injure her, dies—it is the law, stronger even than my power. And for the safety of the Nantia I, Ag, ruler of these western lands, am responsible."

"What will you do?" Watkins asked, when he had got the sense of this declaration, from which he saw that safety of the woman was indeed a matter of vital importance to these people.

"Take you three to Kir-Asa for trial before the council of five," Ag said.

"Then we are prisoners here?" Watkins questioned, his hand again straying toward the revolver butt. Ag saw the movement, and interpreted it in the light of Watkins' definition of the revolver.

"Nay," he said hastily, "use no magic, no charms. The fate of the Nantia and her beasts is proof of your power."

"We are prisoners here?" Watkins reiterated.

"So I must hold you," Ag confessed, "yet, given your promise to offer no resistance, still guests also. Kinsman Philip—" and even I could feel the emotion in his appeal—"your coming in this fashion has moved me to lay my house open to you, to give you place as kin and friend. If by your magic you attempt escape, even though it be by the way you came, my own life is forfeit to the council. For it is known to my household, and beyond, that you three have come through the pass to me, and that the Nantia and many of her beasts have suffered death in a way strange to our people—death that breaks and mangles bone and flesh beyond the power of spear thrusts. As you are in my hands, so am I in your hands, yet I will trust you in freedom among my people until the time of trial, if you will."

Watkins considered. "Nobly spoken, Ag," he said at last. "What would you have us do?"

"I myself cannot pass sentence on my guests," Ag said, and by that Watkins knew that the age-old bond of hospitality which runs among unspoiled people from Tangier to Singapore was sacred in the eyes of these people too. "Thus I would take you to Kir-Asa, and there, chief among your judges, render your sentence light as may be. That is, for the two who are accessory—for the slayer there is no hope."

"None are accessory," Watkins replied. "We three

66

came as one—as one we bear and suffer for each other, fight for each other, and at need die for each other."

I saw Eve watching him with growing approval and admiration. Ag signified his approval more definitely.

"Hear, my son, how the men of our race should always speak," he said. "This is a man."

"Ag," said Watkins—he took the decision on himself, without consulting us who could not understand what was passing—"we will come with you to Kir-Asa. Our magic and your power may yet win us pardon."

But Ag shook his head doubtfully. "There could be no greater crime in the eyes of the people than this of killing the Nantia," he said, "though I realise it as an act to which you were driven by utter peril of life. Kinsman Philip, I take your word, for yourself and Jack and Ce Cil. Rest as my guests, regarded innocent until judgment be made, and free of all that is mine until we set out for Kir-Asa."

With that for a final word he broke up our gathering. I knew little of the gravity of the discussion—or rather, I put it aside from my mind until Watkins should explain its purpose—and lingered over parting with Eve, though I wondered at her expression of grave concern. As soon as we three were alone in our sleeping apartment, Watkins outlined the conversation as nearly as he could. We had small lamps, fed with an oil which, though thicker than paraffin, smelt decidedly like that fuel, and by the light of these we sat to discuss the situation.

"It's a pretty little mess," Watkins concluded, "but we've faced worse. In any case, we must go on to Kir-Asa—Ag has played the man with us, and it's up to us to play the man with him."

And, long though we talked over it, there was really no more to be said. But I think our sleep was none the worse for knowing that trial, with possibly sentence of death as a verdict, waited us in the near future. Obviously we had Ag's protection, and we who had faced the dangers of the great gulf and fought the monkey guard were not to be greatly daunted by a thing we could foresee, and in which we could to a certain extent count on aid. Our view was that we had faced and overcome dangers as great as this, though of

67

a different kind; perhaps the episodes of the past fortnight made us over-confident, and yet it seems to me that in our position we could not have too much confidence.

Be that as it may, Watkins' sly allusions to Eve got home on me more than his statement of our coming trial. I was with him fully when he told how he had declined to hold one of us more responsible than the others for the death of the monkey woman, and as a matter of course was with him in the decision to go to Kir-Asa with Ag—there could be no other decision.

"Of course, Faulkner," he commented, "you'll be glad to get back here when the trouble has blown over, and there'll be a welcome for you, too. Never saw quite such rapid progress, as far as I can remember."

He dodged the boot I threw at him, and bobbed up again. "Bad shot—these affairs of the heart generally make the hand unsteady. Well, I was young myself, once."

In the morning he wakened me by whistling snatches of "Salut d'Amour" and the "Bridal Chorus" in my ear, continuing until I got up and chased him round the room, belabouring him with my hard pillow. Bent sat up and grinned approval, but did not join in. At last Watkins sat down on his bed.

"I can understand your good spirits, Faulkner," he said, "but on the whole I think that for men awaiting sentence of death Bent and I are remarkably cheerful."

I was moved to serious questioning for a minute. "Then you don't really attach much importance to the possibilities of the trial?" I asked.

He shook his head doubtfully. "Ag is a good man, and we are good men," he said. "What is against us we have yet to find out. For the rest, to-day is good—if we could have foreseen the path through the gorge, or the monkey fight, we should have been scared pale green—and we pulled through. Now let's tell ourselves that we shall pull through again, and we shall pull through."

It was good, Khayyamish philosophy, rather damped by Ag's gravity when he came to conduct us to breakfast. Eve and the boy Ner were there to eat with us, but Niala, Ag's wife, did not appear. We began the meal as a sober party, taking our note from our host, but Watkins, who knew a few conjuring tricks, produced a knife from the back of his neck, took a sweet potato from Bent's ear, and with these and two or three more bits of elementary magic—of which he was careful to explain the secrets—won a smile or two from Eve and laughter from the boy. After that Ag understood that we were not unduly depressed; the air cleared, and we passed to the easy, pleasant footing of the preceding evening.

We learned that Ag had his town residence in Kir-Asa, where, as head of the governing council, he spent about half his time. He proposed to set out with us, taking his family as was his custom, the next morning, devoting two days to the journey. Having explained this to Watkins, he handed us over to the boy Ner, who would show us anything we wished to see in connection with the estate.

I had made such progress in the language that when Watkins told me of this, I was able to invite Eve to accompany us. The invitation consisted of the one word "Come?" put questioningly. She accepted. Though Ner guided us painstakingly and courteously, I learned little from our inspection, but improved my vocabulary.

The way of such intimacies as mine with Eve is easy to follow, easy to foretell. Whether, at that time, her brown eyes lighted all the world for me, or whether the full realisation of unquestioning surrender to the spell of love came later, I cannot tell, looking back from this point to that day. I know that already this queenly girl was stirring me to folly—for, alien in speech and far separated in training, habits, conceptions of life, as we were, it was folly from a practical standpoint—and already I was past resistance, content in the present and careless for the future, glad that of us three she devoted her attention most to me. I did not know, then, that on her side there was an ulterior motive for encouraging me. Later I learned that when Watkins told of our exploits on the way, and caused her to regard us as heroes capable of slaying any dragons, she turned to the one of us whom instinctive liking bade her choose, and regarded me as an instrument with which to dispose of her particular dragon. More of that in its place.

Her motive, her initial reason for accepting my advances so readily, was innocent enough, and when I came to know the whole matter it made no difference in my regard for her. At that time, not knowing, I was very well pleased that she should constitute herself my instructress in the language of the country, and generally attach herself more to me than to Bent or Watkins.

That night Watkins forbore to chaff. He sat on his bed with a boot in his hand, and regarded me.

"This looks serious, Faulkner," he said. "I'd be first to admit that she's a charming girl, but you're making a pace that will land you in John Watkins' position very soon, if you're not careful."

"Possibly," I said. "I could imagine a worse fate."

He whistled. "Jack Faulkner, you're twenty-nine, old enough to be a little wiser. One wakes from dreams, remember,"

"Does it matter, if the dreams come true?" I asked.

He sat and mused, absently. "If it's the big thing," he said at last, "may the gods be good to both of you, and it's no man's work to interfere. If I hadn't let the big thing go when I might have held it, I shouldn't be wandering all over the East for things to help me to forget—I shouldn't be here. I let it go, and that's my own little tragedy—you've got to decide for yourself whether to let go or hold. Only—I like these people, and they come a little nearer to me than pure-blooded foreigners, as you know. Don't play, Faulkner."

Whatever may have been my realisation of Eve before, I know that his request then forced me to face the situation. "It's not play, Watkins," I told him.

He put his boot down on the floor carefully, came over to me, and put a hand on my shoulder. "If I can help old chap, let me know," he said.

Somehow the simple request brought us immeasurably nearer to each other. I think it was his breadth of outlook, his lack of prejudice such as a smaller man might have displayed in a like case, and his implicit reliance on my sense of honour, that strengthened the bond between us. I felt, to put it mildly, grateful to him; he might have ridiculed, or condemned; instead, he understood.

In this was one of the examples of how Bent was

apart from us two. He lay on his bed, listening, but making no attempt at comment or participation in something—not an unimportant thing in its possible bearing on our future—which Watkins and I shared. His separateness then was characteristic of our intercourse after the shooting in the pass, and, judging Watkins and myself as impartially as possible, I cannot see it as all our fault. Of his own volition he held away from us; he did not take the matter of the coming trial as lightly as did we, and I think the fact that he was responsible weighed on him.

We had had no hint of the nature of our journey to Kir-Asa, and next morning we found it something of a state affair. There were wooden wheeled, springless rickshaws with cane bodies to convey us along the great road, with two men to pull each one of us. In addition to this staff Ag took some two score of his multitudinous servants. We set out early, an imposing procession headed by the white-attired major-domo, and made a long halt in the middle of the day to avoid its greatest heat. Our way lay through an area of unvarying fertility, well watered, and apparently cultivated with great care. Our noon halt was made under a big, reed-roofed, open shelter beside the road, and here a cloth was spread on the ground and food set out by the retinue Ag had brought. Nightfall brought us to a little group of reed huts, which we learned were specially constructed—as was the midday shelter—for Ag's journeys between his country estate and city residence.

That evening I found I had made great progress in the language. I could understand some of the talk between Watkins and Ag, and as we all ate together again Eve gave me further tuition. When we three got to the hut apportioned to us, Watkins showed his appreciation of my knowledge.

"What's the word for 'understanding,' Watkins?" I asked him.

"You're not in my class," he answered, "and I'll stuff you no more. Ask your own instructor to-morrow."

And, though I pressed the query, he was obdurate.

"I'm going to sleep," he announced finally. "My pronunciation isn't perfect, anyhow, and the word's a tough one in their language. You go to sleep too, Adam. She'll fix that word for you to-morrow, and as many more as you care to ask."

I was just dozing off when his voice came to waken me.

"In your shoes, I wouldn't care if I didn't know their old language," he said. "It's a fine, healthy sort of excuse."

In the silence that followed I had nearly gone off to sleep, when:

"What about retaliating with lessons in English? They might be useful, later on."

The darkness of the hut, the hint of amusement in his voice, and my own realisation of all the suggestion implied, come back to me as I write.

In the morning we set out again along the great paved road, passing on toward the smoke column that went up from the volcano directly ahead of us, behind Kir-Asa itself—the smoke was less in volume, I thought, than when we had seen it from a greater distance. The crater and bare, upper slopes were clearly visible at about twenty miles' distance from where we set out that morning. We were still passing through a district of well-tended, irrigated fields of maize, areas of plantain growth, and enclosures of grass land on which small, dun-coloured, humped cattle grazed. These cattle and multitudes of pigs comprised the domestic animals of the country—both sheep and horses were unknown, and I saw no goats; the pigs were generally dirty white, though there was a black breed as well, and intermediates; they were all long-legged, scrawny brutes, but the pork left nothing to be desired.

At near on noon the way began to ascend. Soon the ground on either side grew arid and rocky, except where water had been led down from some still higher ground beyond to make vegetation possible. There were some ugly cactus growths in this belt, and Ag told us that their fibres were used for the making of fine linen. Ahead of us a great rock wall showed, cutting directly across our line of travel; it was about twenty-five feet in height, with the top overhanging toward us, and, when we could see both sides, we found that the thickness of the top of the wall was about a third greater than that of its base, so that it overhung on both sides.

On the side nearer to us a trench or moat, about twenty feet in depth and width, went down from the base of the wall. Moat and wall formed the defences of Kir-Asa, and to any attack without artillery the place was utterly impregnable. From the bottom of the moat to the top of the wall the distance was at no point less than forty feet, and this great fortification had not been built; it had been hewn from the solid rock, as had the whole city. The founders of this place had chosen a site where the quality of the rock over a large area admitted of enduring results from their work, and here they had quarried them a city which, I estimated later, could house half a million people in comfort within its protecting wall.

The diameter of the city, roughly circular in plan, was somewhere between two and three miles. Toward the point where the road passed through the wall our servants pulled us up a fairly steep ascent, and we saw that there were two square apertures in the wall itself to give entrance to the city. These were closed at need by circles of rock fitted in grooves, like gigantic pennies stood on edge, and capable of being rolled back into hollows in the wall to give access to the city. A simple mechanism of levers, actuated from the inside, controlled these unique gates. The squared holes in the wall into which they fitted to close the way into the city were about twenty feet in height. As we passed through the right-hand aperture—I saw the edge of the great stone towering high in its recess on my right hand, while the slot into which it fitted below ground, so as completely to close the square hole when required, was spanned by stout wooden planks over which our conveyances were pulled.

Before us a wide avenue led straight across half the city to its centre; on either side of it the quarried edifices rose to flat tops that were level with the top of the wall, for the most part, though some were a few feet higher. It must be understood that there was no building, practically, as we understand the word, in Kir-Asa; the whole city was quarried out of the solid rock.

Yet it was not gloomy or unpleasing. There were open spaces to which soil had been brought of sufficient depth to support palms and graceful flowering shrubs, as well as the lighter growth which the climate and nature of the soil forced to a gorgeous profusion. From lack of care many of these beds had withered and died, for the people who now inhabited the city were like a spider living in a tortoise-shell—they filled barely a fortieth part of the whole; the rest was unused, neglected, almost unvisited.

Ag pointed up the avenue to a great mansion that stood in the centre of the city. "The house of the king," he said, and Watkins translated for our benefit. So far as I was concerned, he need not have taken the trouble—but I did not tell him so.

There were many people in this main street; women, clad similarly to Eve and her mother, but in varying degrees of fineness, stopped to watch us pass; men looked, and then paused at the unfamiliar attire and pale faces of Ag's three guests. And there were children, inquisitive as children are in every country, who ran beside our rickshaws, got in the way of Ag's attendants, or peered out at us from the pillared porticoes with which many of the buildings (for so I must call them, for want of a better word) were fronted.

We turned in at a great mansion that stood half-way between the city gateway and the king's house, descending from our conveyances at the entrance, and passing to a spacious hall which rose to the full height of the mansion, and boasted two rows of square columns as intermediate supports for the rock roof. Apartments opened out on either side, and at the far end from the entrance a splendid stairway of quartz led to galleries which gave access to the rooms of the two upper stories. This central hall and division of the space on either side into three floors was typical of the majority of the mansions of Kir-Asa. Later we found it reproduced on a far more magnificent scale in the house of the king.

"My guests," said Ag, "I bid you welcome to my house."

So we came to Kir-Asa.

A messenger had preceded Ag, so that when we entered the mansion all was prepared for us. We three were conducted to the first gallery of the mansion, and found that a suite of four communicating rooms had been apportioned to us. Here we removed all traces of our journey, and an obsequious servitor, waiting in the gallery, preceded us back to the great central hall, where on a dining table of solid stone, we joined Ag and his family and one other for the midday meal.

"My kinsman and his friends," Ag introduced us, adding our names. To us he named the newcomer as "Ahan-Neray," which immediately told us not only that the man was Neray son of Ahan, but also that he was eldest or only son of his father, since only in the case of the eldest son was this compound form of name used. Had he been a second son—though few families boasted more than one—he would have been introduced as "Neray of the house of Ahan," but the two names would not have been spoken in conjunction with each other.

"That man," Watkins remarked to me, "has got to name his son Ahan, whether he likes it or no. Pretty hard on him."

The man Neray was about my own height—that is, just six feet—and something of a dandy in his way. He wore a braided leather belt, while Ag and Ner were content with plain leather, and his belt clasp of yellow metal was set with such bits of green crystal—emerald—as Niala and Eve wore for necklaces. We did not yet know these stones for emeralds, but I guessed the clasp to be gold, and I was right.

He was darker of skin than Niala; had his hair not been cut quite so closely, and had his nose been a bit longer, one might have taken him for a Pathan horse-dealer—he inclined rather to that type, and it is a kingly breed of men, in appearance. When we sat down to our meal I sat on the left of Ag, who took the centre seat on one side of the stone table; Eve sat on my left, and Neray, with a somewhat hostile stare at me as if I had usurped his place, made a conspicuous promenade of going to sit by Niala. It was easy to see the state of affairs as far as he was concerned; as for

Eve, it seemed to me that she had an extra welcoming smile for me.

"My kinsmen are strangers," Ag told Neray. "They come from a land, through the great cleft beyond our western border."

Neray considered it. "The Nantia gave you safe passage?" he asked me.

"The Nantia is dead," Watkins answered for me.

Neray stared. "But the new Nantia——?" he asked and hesitated.

"Is already on her way to her task," Ag replied. "That is my concern, Neray." Then he put all the cards on the table with regard to us. "These my guests have come to Kir—Asa to stand before the council of five and answer for the Nantia's death."

He spoke slowly, and I got the whole of the sentence with little difficulty. I saw Eve's hand steal along the settee toward me as if she would assure me of her sympathy; she did not check the involuntary movement in time to prevent Neray's seeing it.

Ag's statement was like the dropping of a bomb. Neray's jaw dropped, and he stared aghast at me, opposite to him. Here was a thing incredible to him.

"Slayers of the Nantia—free in my city?" he gasped.

"Not so, Neray," Ag said composedly, "but my kinsman and his friends, not yet judged, and therefore by law not to be held guilty of the slaying, for aught we know. Freely and of their own will came they with me to Kir-Asa, and if you are governor of the city, yet am I head of the council."

From that I knew not only that Neray was governor of the city, but also that as member of the council of five he would be one of our judges. His evident jealousy over Eve's partiality for me might prove a factor in his judgment of the case, I felt. As Ag's guest, he made no further protest against the leniency with which we were treated.

"When will the trial be held?" he asked.

"I am summoning the council to meet on the fourth day from this, in mid-morning," Ag answered. "Word has gone out to the remaining three lords, and there are some small matters of state that need adjustment. This trial will follow on our decisions of state concerns."

76

Watkins, eyeing the clasp on Neray's belt, changed the subject. "Tell me, Ag," he asked, "where do you smelt that metal?"

But Ag could not understand the question. Watkins explained to him that all metals are diffused in rocks, and smelted out by heat or some refining process. Neray grinned his incredulity, and even Ag looked doubtful over the news.

"Whence do you obtain your metals, then?" Watkins asked.

"From the storehouses of Kir-Asa," Neray answered, with a rather pitying smile, as if it were an obvious matter.

"Yet for your spears, your spades, your knives, and all the metal articles you use, such stores must soon be exhausted," Watkins commented.

Ag smiled. "If ten times our number drew on the stores for twenty times the life of a man, they would not use half the blocks of metal here," he said. "As for that yellow clasp, though it will not rust it is a soft metal, of little use save for the making of ornaments, and the stores of it are but meagre—they would scarce fill half this hall. But of the white metal—the blocks are eaten with rust in some chambers, it is true, yet there is all that the people need for generations to come."

I had a vision of gold ingots, enough to "scarce fill half this hall," lying unvalued in this city of a trebly guarded land. I imagined them passing the barrier of the great gulf to upset the metal markets of the world—gold by the thousand tons! Meanwhile it was apparent that this race had never smelted a single ton of ore; its people drew on stores left by some extinct predecessors and sufficient for all their simple needs.

"Have you no mines?" Watkins asked.

"What are mines?" Neray asked in reply.

Watkins explained, as well as he was able. Both Ag and Neray pleaded their country's innocence of such—the idea of metal having to be won from rock seemed incomprehensible to them, though Ag confessed that up toward the volcano there was a hole in the ground whence they won oil, such as was used in their lamps—it was thicker than the lamp fuel, and they had a crude process of distillation to refine it.

77

"Do you not use stone for building?" Watkins asked, trying to find if there were any quarrying, such as would have given a hint of the existence of metal in rock strata.

"Why should we build, save for reed huts that the people erect as they need?" Ag asked him in return. "Are there not enough of houses in the land?"

"Good Lord!" Watkins muttered in English. "Here's a race that has taken over a country ready-made—no mines and no buildings—no nice little flutters on a toy stock exchange, and not a solitary bricklayer to form a trade union and demand a minimum wage. Do you get it, Faulkner?"

"I'd like to see the gold reserve," I answered.

"I cannot understand," Neray remarked, inviting translation.

"I told my friend what you have told me," Watkins said to him.

"It takes many words in your tongue to express few in ours," Neray remarked suspiciously.

"That gentleman is asking for a thick ear," Watkins said to me. Then: "You have money—tokens for the barter of goods?" he asked Ag.

"For little things—yes," Ag answered, and took from a pocket in his tunic a disk of white metal, on which was stamped, or rather sunk, the device of an axe on one side. The reverse of the coin was plain.

"These are for small things," he said, "and we set their value against a measure of maize. But for larger transactions they are too heavy, and a man will give pigs for an ox, eggs for maize, meat for clothing, or for boots. It is easier."

"And if a man would buy land?" Watkins asked.

"Buy land?" Ag echoed, as if Watkins spoke of carrying water in a sieve. "The land is the property of us four lords of the provinces and of our children, save for that portion which belongs to the king."

"But the people who till the land—what hold have they?"

Ag found our ignorance, of a system which, to himself was as immutable as the laws of life and death, amusing.

"Each man holds land from his lord," he said, "and renders part of its fruits to his lord for the use of the
78

land. Thus are all fed, and all content—there is enough for all."

The ideal, patriarchal simplicity of such a system!

"No water rate, no income tax," Watkins remarked to me.

"And this race of yours—for how many generations has it held the land?" he asked next.

"Generations beyond numbering," Ag answered. "Ages since, it was a great and powerful race, spreading beyond these borders, but for generations the race has dwindled—the children are few. Before this was a race of another sort, and before that again a people of which little is known save that they cut this city out of the rock, and that their king lived in another, greater city, far away in the West. They have left writings of which some two or three were translated and also written in the language of our first fathers here—none can read the writing of that first people now."

So this, the third race in succession to possess so desirable a heritage, was dying out. I found later that Ag and his son and daughter were on the whole more vigorous, mentally stronger, than the pure breed, in which, taking them in the mass, was a lack of initiative, disinclination to enterprise, typified in the fact that with no great show of force four "lords" could parcel out the country between them and hold its population as serfs, albeit comfortable serfs. We met individuals active and enterprising enough in the ruling class among which fate and Ag's help had fixed our lot, but it appeared that the race as a whole had inherited too much, lost the initiative and constructive genius that comes of being forced to self-dependence.

Watkins questioned further, and found that the decrease in population had long been a cause for concern. It had even led to modification of the laws affecting marriage.

"If two of our people marry and have no children by the end of the fourth year," Ag told him, "then they may go their ways unquestioned to marry others, but in such case the man is forced to marry again, lest he should leave his wife without just cause."

"Why only the man—why is not the woman compelled also?" Watkins asked.

"There is no need," Ag told him, evidently amused

at the idea. "For every four girl children that are born there are five men children, and the woman in such a case would have no peace."

"Solution of the problem of the surplus woman—export her here," Watkins remarked to me. These asides of his were texts with which I could freshen his memory afterwards, so that he could amplify what I had understood of the conversation.

We learned much of the ways of the country at that meal, for which it seemed that Neray had dropped in in a casual way, calling on his fellow member of the council. His real reason for coming was apparent when he took his leave, for he bent over Eve's hand and spoke softly to her a little apart from the rest of us, and I saw her shake her head at his words. His manner toward me was plainly disdainful, and Eve looked from him to me as if comparing us. . .

Late in the afternoon Ag visited us in our rooms, and Watkins assured him that we had everything we could wish, and were more than comfortable. Then Ag, evidently with a weight on his mind, sat down to consult us—or rather, to confer with Watkins.

"I would seek your advice, kinsman Philip," he began, a little nervously for him, "and your aid as well, if among your magic there is a charm that will serve."

"All in our power is at your service," Watkins assured him.

"Neray took my daughter apart to tell her the king is dying," Ag said. "This he has told her at many times these past three years, but some day it may be true."

"Probably it will," Watkins agreed. "But why should the king not die, if he likes?"

"The king has three sons, Comin-Saya, his heir, Manos, and Macer the youngest," Ag proceeded. "While the king lives, these three have not so much power as I hold as head of the council. At the king's death Comin-Saya has power of life and death over me and my house, as would the king hold now if he were sane."

Watkins considered this. "You mean the minute the king dies the new king can do as he likes with you and your belongings?" he suggested.

"It is so," Ag answered—he had no more thought of questioning that absolute power than of doubting the existence of the sun. For these people laws were inexorable.

"Meanwhile the heir to the throne, as such, has no power at all," Watkins continued.

"That is the law," Ag said.

"Well—on what subject do you seek our advice or aid?"

"Comin-Saya, son of Saya-Comin the king, has asked me thrice for my daughter Eve in marriage," Ag explained.

Still Watkins was puzzled, and I understood enough to be worse than puzzled. I saw this business more clearly than did Watkins, having a deeper interest in it.

"Why refuse such an honour?" Watkins asked. "Surely—the king's wife——"

"The king who still lives is mad," Ag interrupted, "and Comin-Saya his father also went mad before him and strangled his wife as she slept beside him, for in madness love becomes hate. It may be that this Comin-Saya, the heir, will in turn go mad, and thus I will not give him the daughter I love."

Watkins thought it over. "If she were already married?" he asked.

"There would then be no need for your charms," Ag said. "I would not drive her to marriage against her will—this Neray, governor of the city, has urged her these five years past, and only to-day he reminded her that the king's death would place her in Comin-Saya's power."

"Is she inclined toward Comin-Saya, think you?" Watkins inquired.

Ag shook his head. "She is of my mind," he answered, "and would sooner die than go to Comin-Saya."

"And Neray—what is her mind about him?" Watkins pursued.

"The mind of a maid—wavering as a leaf in a wind," Ag said. "For years she has held him off, though of all who have sought her he has won most smiles."

Watkins thought it over. "Jack—Cecil," he said at last. "Listen while I state the case," and he gave us the facts as Ag had put them before him, while Ag for his part looked at us hopefully. We listened, and at the end of the recital Bent shook his head.

"Insoluble," was his comment.

I had a thought of asking Ag to let me try my luck against Neray, but would not risk it. Like Bent, I had to shake my head, and again Watkins mused.

"I have it," he announced finally.

"What?" I asked.

He disregarded the query. "Ag," he asked, "of all the lords of this land, and of all people who hold any power, how many incline to you and how many against you?"

Ag balanced one hand against the other as if to say that the count was equal. "Of people who have power there are few in the land," he said, "but full half would do my bidding."

"And who, next to the king, holds most power in the land?" Watkins asked next.

The import of the question dawned on Ag slowly. When he understood, he stood up, staring at Watkins as if unable to believe his ears.

"Yet are you slave to a custom," said Watkins the iconoclast. "A man of strength and no small wisdom, you submit without question to a family that breeds madmen generation by generation, giving them power of life and death over yourself and your children. I tell you there is one way, and only one way, for the saving of Eve your daughter from this fate you fear."

"No," said Ag, as if he would thrust the mere idea out of his mind. "Say no more, kinsman Philip."

"Choose for yourself," Watkins said. "Sacrifice your daughter whom you love, the noblest lady this land has shown us, to Comin-Saya—or take his place."

Ag turned and fled from us, and as he went out Watkins smiled.

I had not understood all of this; when it was explained to me I had not overmuch liking for it. Revolutions had not been part of my training, I pointed out.

"You miss my brilliant idea, my ulterior motive," said Watkins the crafty. "If Ag were king, there'd be an end of the trouble about that infernal monkey woman—we could count on going to the football match on Saturday afternoon without the bother of carrying our heads under our arms. King Ag, with power of life and death—the solution of his troubles

82

and our own as well."

"The trial takes place in three days' time," I reminded him. "Ag is not likely to revolt in so short a time as that."

"I've given him the pill, and he's swallowed it," Watkins retorted. "If only the mad king is really on his last legs, that pill will work—Ag will hop around and get things done. All we can do is to pray for a break in the weather, so that the king's rheumatism gets really painful."

There was not much hope, I felt, as far as evading trial was concerned, and, from the attitude of Neray, for whom I had little liking, there would be one of the five judges dead against us. Meanwhile, I had three days in which to get on with learning the language, just in case I might have a use for it after the trial.

That evening, when we met round the table for food, there were no outsiders present. Ag looked thoughtful, but made no direct reference to Watkins' daring suggestion. He listened courteously but abstractedly while Watkins told him impossible fairy tales of carriages that ran without men to pull them, and of men talking to each other at a distance equal to the whole stretch of this country. He was tremendously interested, though, when with the aid of the hinged cover to the mirror I had given Eve—and which she carried with her that evening—Watkins explained the principle of hanging doors on hinges instead of lifting them bodily about. In fact, he announced his intention of calling in a craftsman in metal working, explaining the marvel to him, and getting a specimen set of hinges made.

THE CITY OF WONDERS

Before we had risen next morning, Ag's chief servitor came to us bearing suits of the clothing of these people, by his master's order.

"If you choose to go about the city, lords," he said, "my lord bids you accept these poor gifts, that you may escape remark through the strangeness of your attire."

We bade him thank his master for this characteristic

thought for our comfort, and put the things on. They were of the finest linen, and better suited to this warm climate than our own shabby clothes, though I missed my breeches pockets and felt as if I had been put into an old-fashioned nightshirt far too short for me.

"Lord save us!" Watkins ejaculated, when we had all three dressed. "If there's a high wind to-day, I'm staying in."

We all felt a bit nervous at first, but, so far as wind was concerned, the unvarying breeze from the west swept gently enough through the city, and in regard to that I think the volcanic area, causing an up-draught through its warmth, sucked in air toward itself to produce this breeze throughout the small extent of the country in the dry season, in which, except for occasional storms, calm weather was the rule. In the rainy season, due to begin about three months hence, storms of almost more than tropical violence made life in the huts of the peasantry a misery.

We saw nothing of Ag till the evening of that day, nor, was he with us in the daytime for any of the three days before the assembly of the council. From this Watkins augured good results.

"My pill is working," he said. "Ag is rigging the market, and shares in royalty aren't worth buying."

As to that, we had to wait on events. Meanwhile Niala, solicitous as her husband for our well-being—she was a sort of neutral echo of Ag—suggested that both Ner and Eve would show us anything we cared to see of the city. To me it seemed strange that a girl like Eve should be permitted such freedom with strangers, but here, since for the sake of race they were of such immense importance, women had equal freedom with men in every way, in addition to the privileges their sex conferred. In Kir-Asa a man would as soon think of killing his father as of offering insult to a woman, and the penalties for both offences would be about equal. As an illustration of this, one night when Ag went to Neray's house, which stood beyond the king's palace in the centre of the city, Niala went unattended to join him through the unlighted street, and there was no moon. She would have smiled at the idea of requiring a male escort.

The absence of personal property, as we understand

it was largely responsible for this state of affairs. Although theft was not unknown, in a country where, as Ag put it, there was enough for all, half the dangers of what we are pleased to call civilised life were absent. The ways of the people were more those of the Inca kingdom of Peru than any other I can recall.

In those three days we saw much. We began by going up to the centre of the city, where in the middle of a great circular space stood the hewn palace of the kings of Kir-Asa. In front of the palace itself was a gigantic monolith, square in section and perfectly plain. Its face was about eight feet in width, as one looked toward the palace, and with its lower edge about on a level with my eyes a tablet of gold, some five feet square, was blended into the rock. At the top of the tablet was an axe engraved as a sort of heraldic device, and under this were characters not unlike Chinese writing, occupying about three-quarters of the tablet. Under this inscription, as it proved to be, was a translation into the written characters of this people's language—it was another Rosetta stone, a key to the language of the world's first civilisation.

Here Eve and the boy led us first, and we gazed at the monolith, towering above us to the height of the city wall.

"This," said Ner, "is the work of him who hewed the city."

Watkins looked up at the inscription. "Can you read it for us?" he asked.

"Assuredly," Ner said, "since that small writing at the foot of the tablet is in our own language."

He read it out. Later, I got Eve to read it to me again, slowly, and I wrote it down. If only as proof of the vanity of human pride, and the impermanence of fame, it is worth recording:

"A decree of Kirtas-Asen, viceroy of the isles and lands of the East, holder of the second sceptre, warden of the eastern gate, lord of slaves unnumbered, terrible in war, and in my rule just to all the people.

"In this tenth year of my viceroyalty was hewed the last chamber of this city of my pride, and was laid the last stone of the road that runs twenty days' journey to the sea. I have filled all the storehouses of this my city with gold and corn and the metals of war and of peace, and have made provision of water, so that if the whole earth shall fail of her fruits there shall be no lack nor any need that shall not be met in this city of my pride.

"Now I in my pride decree:

"As Kir the mountain of fire that is set over this city bears witness to the glory of my father Kirtas who was viceroy of the isles and warden of the eastern gate before me, so shall the name of this city in token of my glory be called Kir-Asa while the generations of men endure. So throughout all the world for ever shall the sons of men bow down at the speaking of my name, because of my glory and my pride.

"At the rising of the sun, O ye peoples of the isles and lands of the East, bow yourselves in honour of the mighty king who sits enthroned in glory in the mother of hewn cities, even An, where is gathered all power that goes forth to rule the world. At the going down of the sun, O peoples, bow yourselves in reverence to me, Kirtas-Asen, who have caused ten thousand slaves to labour that this great city and the road my father Kirtas planned might be perfected in this tenth year of my viceroyalty.

"Thus I in my pride decree, that all the world may know of Kirtas-Asen, whose face is as the sun at noon for its brightness, and whose rule is just to all the peoples, that they may bow themselves before me, and that the glory of my name may be told throughout the world for ever."

The stupendous, unquestioned majesty of that arrogant decree robbed even Watkins of his usual cynical comment. One had but to look at the stately beauty of the city, and in thought to re-people it with the multitudes who once trod its hewn avenues, to realise that its founder had some cause for his magnificent challenge to eternity.

"What must 'An, the mother of hewn cities,' have been?" I questioned.

Eve smiled at me, and I realised what I had done. It was a simple sentence, and unconsciously I had spoken it in her language. Part of my attempts at mastery of the language consisted in putting my unspoken thoughts into its words, and with no other task to occupy me I was making amazing progress.

" 'An,' I take it, was the capital of Atlantis," Watkins commented, "and it must have been such a city as the modern world has never dreamed. They held life and labour cheaply in their day—I can imagine those 'slaves by the ten thousand' quarrying away here, and the overseers with their whips."

"And the jubilation when all was done," Bent added.

We stood in silence for awhile. The terms of that majestic, magniloquent decree were like the coupled music of some great organ, and I felt myself no longer heir of the ages, but a puny mite, son of a weakling age compared with that of the men who hewed Kir-Asa the mighty and laid that enduring road with the stones they took away.

Watkins went up and rubbed the corner of the tablet. The centuries had thinned the gold, but still the decree of Kirtas-Asen showed clear in the quaint characters of his time. The gold itself was not set in the stone in any fashion we know and practise, but in some way was melted in, the metal and stone blended into one fabric—the edge of the tablet was a sort of vignetting, gold fading to grey rock.

"They were a wonderful people," I remarked. "They had a written language, knew the uses of metals, had a definite system of government over all the known world, obviously were good navigators——"

"I've noticed one thing in which they beat the Roman civilisation," Watkins observed. "Rome built aqueducts—these people knew that water finds its own level. In the stone piping in Ag's house, the water comes down from somewhere—the pipe slants upward to the baths."

We found a replica of this tablet, later, blended into the rock wall of the great central hall in the king's house, indicating that it had been the palace of Kirtas-Asen in his pride. From beyond the palace the avenue continued to the farther wall of the city, while a second great highway at right angles to this combined with it to cut Kir-Asa into four equal sections. For its full length this second great avenue was bordered on both sides by windowless, single-chambered erections, the storehouses of which the viceregal decree made mention; these storehouses were massive oblongs with circular stone doors that rolled back into their walls like those of the city's gateway.

"Look," said Watkins, and pointed up to a recessed panel over one of these doorways. The panel was carved with a design of wheat-ears, and this people among whom we had come had never known wheat or its uses. The storehouse, about ninety feet in depth by sixty in width, and as high as the wall of the city, was empty, as we found by going inside. The solid rock roof was supported on three rows of plain pillars; the whole appeared to have been excavated from the solid—we could find no trace of any stone having been laid.

"This place is past wondering at," Watkins said. "It makes the Pyramids seem mere jerry-building."

We went out. Watkins and Ner led the way, Bent followed them, and for an instant I lingered with Eve in the shadow beyond the open door. We spoke no word—there was no more between us than a glance of eyes that spoke the story on which the world is based, and, questioning, won the reply desired. It was a definite stage in our intimacy, an advance that could not have been more clearly marked by spoken words. Then, the good moment passed, we followed silently where the others had gone.

It may be unique that Eve admitted, without seeking to retract, these advances—she was above coquetry, in spite of the mischievous gaiety that lighted some of her moods. I am biassed with regard to her, but from the first she seemed to me to possess some of the breadth of outlook, the fineness of character, that marked Watkins and made me admire him. There was nothing small about Eve, no petulance, nor indecision; knowing a thing—even this—she admitted the knowledge freely; she was above subterfuge, and would have made a poor conspirator.

In another of the great storehouses we visited, hexagonal ingots of corroded metal still occupied three-fourths of the interior. I scratched an ingot, and found that in the dryness of this place the corrosion had been but slight—under it showed the white alloy of which the head of the spear I had brought had been forged, but these ingots were soft and untempered. The metal was used by the smiths of the country for practically all its needs; there had been stores of iron as well, but rust had eaten it all away and left great masses of scaly, powdery oxide, which the present race left untouched, as of no use to them. I concluded that the white alloy was the "metal of peace" mentioned in the vaunting decree, while iron would be the "metal of war."

"What are you thinking, Faulkner?" Watkins asked as we stood in the white metal storehouse. It was one of several—we entered three—and there were thousands of tons of the stuff, still untouched.

"I was wondering what Kirtas-Asen would say if he could come back and see this weak little people, cut off from all the world, occupying his city and forgetting to do reverence to his pride," I said.

"He'd swear, hard," Watkins affirmed confidently "and I'd like to hear him."

He gave me a thought, and I turned to Eve:

"What are your gods?" I asked.

It was a subject on which we had not thought to touch before. She bowed her head in reverence at mention of the word. "The twin gods, lords of life and death, Oneta and Rak," she said. "Three days are set apart each year, after the gathering of the maize harvest, for their worship."

"And you believe in a life after this?" I questioned again.

"Of course," she answered with a smile. "Why else should we live here? Beyond the stars all live again."

There was a ritual, as simple as her unquestioning faith, which was used for the three sacred days of the year, and much singing. But—a good point—there was no priestly order; the five lords of the council were responsible to the king for knowledge of the ritual being maintained, and for the observance of the sacred period, and there the matter ended. It was natural; a contented, pastoral and agricultural people had no need to propitiate the gods overmuch, and thus there was little incentive to a complication of rites and observances.

One other storehouse—we visited it last in our tour of inspection of the transverse avenue—demands mention. It stood near the centre of the city, in the angle where this avenue intersected the other and was broken by the space surrounding the royal house. It was comparatively small, about thirty feet by twenty, and not more than fifteen feet from floor to roof, with one central row of supporting columns. It was not quite half-filled with hexagonal bars of soft, pure gold, each about twenty pounds in weight, as nearly as I could judge.

We gazed in utter, almost stupefied silence. Here, as Ag had told us, was gold by the thousand tons—Kirtas-Asen must have ransacked the world, and yet probably at "An, the mother of hewn cities" the store had been greater still. It lay unvalued, useless, such a treasure as no men have seen before or since—I thought then that if we got back to the coast we might take a couple of bars apiece across the trembling bridge and up the ledge of the great chasm, but no more. Kir-Asa could give us wealth beyond any man's imaginings, but we could not move it from the place.

"From this metal our smiths fashion ornaments," Eve told us, "but it is too heavy and too soft for the uses of our people. It endures the passing of time without rust."

What a comment, I thought, on the futility of avarice! We stood before the greatest treasure in the world, by our standards, and because of its weight and softness "a bar of it wouldn't buy a duck's egg, here," as Watkins put it.

We passed to streets faced by dwellings of hewn quartz, magnificent, desolate, with fragments of the stone from their carvings lying unheeded in the empty ways: there were great carven-fronted mansions, unused, with gaping doorways and dust inches thick on their floors; there were open spaces with withered and deserted gardens, and statuary of which the design had been worn and rounded from its original intent by the winds and rains of countless centuries. For the three days before the assembly of the council we explored, finding new wonders at every turn, and wearying Ner and Eve by our persistent questioning. One thing struck me—there were no tombs; the present race cremated its dead, the custom being possibly a legacy from the wonderful civilisation that had produced Kir-Asa the mighty.

In one of the deserted open places, surrounded by pillared palaces of magnificent design, I paused with Eve beside me to look round.

"This would look wonderful by moonlight," I said, realising how the softer light of night would cover all traces of decay. But Eve shook her head.

"None come to the deserted places by night," she said.

"Why not?" I asked.

But she looked at me in a distressed way without replying, and I recalled how both she and her mother had looked when Watkins spoke of the apparitions of the valley amphitheatre. Did the "ghosts who chase women" haunt the dead quarters of this city too, I wondered?

The last night but one before the trial, Bent, sitting on his bed, gave vent to his thoughts.

"How long do we stay here, Watkins?" he asked.

"Till after our trial," Watkins answered reflectively. "Why?"

"I was wondering what we get out of it, after all," Bent said.

"So far as you are concerned," Watkins retorted, "you get what I agreed to pay you when we made our bargain, and in addition to that you can have as much gold as you care to carry away."

Bent made a sort of hopeless gesture. "How do you think we'll get away?" he asked. "The way we came?"

"Certainly not," Watkins answered bitingly. "I'm asking Ag to-morrow to have a tunnel driven straight from here to Singapore. We're to be shot through it by pneumatic pressure, like those cash delivery systems in department stores."

Bent looked furious—I could not restrain a laugh.

"Ah, well!" he said, "if one of you simply means to play the fool with a woman while the other dodders round mouldy antiquities, I've no more to say."

"That," Watkins said, "is our loss. Good-night, Bent."

I looked for an explosion, but Bent lay down to sleep without deigning to reply.

The next night we were very quiet over our meal. The boy Ner did most of the talking; the rest of us felt the coming ordeal weigh heavily on us. Ag was unusually kindly and courteous, even for him, and specially attentive to me. I could converse with him now with tolerable freedom, and I noticed how he referred to Eve's tuition and its results, complimenting me on my quickness. After the meal, he did not leave us to go out, as was his custom, but went instead to one of the apartments giving on to the great central hall, and signed to me to follow.

I entered the room for the first time. Its stone floor was covered with skins, its settees were comfortably padded and had raised ends which formed back rests, and altogether it was the most luxurious room of all that I had seen. A dozen or so of the oil lamps that these people used diffused light on its fittings.

"Jack, son of Faulk," Ag began boldly enough, "I am not a blind man."

"Far from it," I said.

"You are a stranger, a man of magic, but in you I see a man of truth."

There was no possible reply to the compliment that I could think of—for such it was, though obviously Ag was not talking for the sake of complimenting me.

"I have no liking for the plan of Philip my kinsman. In it is danger, and should it fail my house is doomed. Yet the king is very near to death, and my daughter Eve is very dear to me."

Again I kept silence, though Ag seemed to wait reply.

"If I gave her to any man, betrothal would save her from Comin-Saya, should the king die," he explained. "I know the trial waits you with the morn, but as head of the council I might save one, or two."

"We three are as one," I answered readily enough now. "As one we came and as one we stand."

Ag hesitated. "Or I might save three," he said slowly. Perhaps the offer was put forward without any hope of being able to fulfil it, to win my consent to his plan, and perhaps he hoped to save us all.

I nodded. "We three are as one," I said again.

He let it pass. "If of her own desire—I am not blind Jack son of Faulk—if of her own desire Eve my daughter were held betrothed to you, and so known if the king should die . . ."

He waited, wondering if I understood the proposal clearly. I thought of Eve as she had been with me these past three days, of Eve transported from this hidden land to an everyday life—in a dozen seconds I saw her in as many different phases, and made decision.

"Then," I said, "her desire would be mine."

Ag looked at me steadily. "To hold and cherish in

92

your own land as in this," he said, "to own and proclaim in disregard of race or inequality of knowledge—life is not play, Jack son of Faulk, and a girl's heart is a fragile thing. To hold thus?"

"More," I answered. "To love, to serve, and to stand beside in pride, Ag, father of Eve."

He looked at me, almost peered into my face, as if questioning me to the uttermost. Then he drew back.

"Wait," he bade, and left me.

Minutes passed while I stood, understanding how Ag planned to gain his end without the risks involved by Watkins' suggestion. In my own mind was no doubt, no questioning; if the trial had not awaited us, if the way to the coast lay open and easy to-morrow, I had no wish to go, leaving Eve behind. As Watkins had phrased it, this was the big thing for me, and I would not let it go.

The rustle of light footsteps on the covered floor sounded as Eve came toward me, her face grave, her steps unhurrying and unfaltering. I stretched out my hands, and she laid her own within them, her eyes downcast. Then she looked up at me for an instant, and wordlessly came closer—I felt her arms go round my neck as I held her. . . .

The shadow of the morrow took away constraint. She nestled close to me, held me as if from the judgment of the council, and to me her love and trust were wonderful.

"Though it be but for this hour, lord of my heart, I am glad," she whispered.

"Have no fear, sweet," I told her. "To-morrow will pass and leave me to love you."

"Here, or beyond the stars," she answered, "as for ever my love is yours. Yet for this hour I would have you hold me close, close, lest another day should find me left with naught but the memory for my gain."

Her whispered, ecstatic sentences come back to me as I write. Only once in life is possible such white passion as made that hour wonderful, and I knew that whatever Kir-Asa held for Bent and Watkins, it had given me all that man could ask.

We went back to the great central hall, my hand on Eve's shoulder, and only Ag and Watkins were there—the rest had gone. Watkins smiled at me—or rather grinned—in his own complacent way. I paused before where Ag sat.

"Daughter of mine," he said, "I give you gladly, if it is your will."

"It is her will," I ventured to speak for her, "as mine. Count not that you lose a daughter, but that here, or half a world away, you are richer by another son."

"My thanks for that," he answered sincerely. "I trust her to you without fear."

When we had got to our own rooms, Watkins grinned at me again.

"Why twist your face about like that?" I asked.

"I can see through Ag's little game," he answered. "Your wish happens to fit in with it. Well, it seems to be the big thing for you, and that being so you have all my good wishes."

"And Ag will not be king," I remarked.

"As to that," Watkins answered deliberately, "we shall see what we shall see. We've got enough to think about to-morrow, anyhow."

BEFORE THE COUNCIL

We put on our own clothes on the morning of the trial; I remarked—the suggestion of discarding native attire and facing the council in our own was mine, because I happened to be first awake—that if things went against us we had a country to be proud of, and might as well own it when we went to our fate.

"Precisely," Watkins agreed.

Before we went down to breakfast he grew grave for a minute. "Boys," he said, "we're hard against it to-day, perhaps, in spite of Ag—he's only one, and we've broken a law that stands for the safety of these people. I'm morally responsible for bringing you here, and I hope to be responsible for taking you back a little richer than you came, somehow. Now one handshake all round before we go to face the music, and may we congratulate each other here this evening—unless Faulkner is otherwise engaged."

He could not resist the final dig at me. I am glad to recall that friendly, cheery handclasp, for which Bent seemed to put aside his aloofness in the knowledge that we two admitted no difference between his position and our own, so far as the coming trial was in question. We had come as one, we stood as one, and in the face of danger Bent felt and owned it.

We breakfasted without Ag, who had gone out early, and without Niala, and afterward Eve and I slipped away for a precious half-hour. Then I heard Bent calling, and left Eve with as good a word of hope as I could contrive, telling her that I would come back to her.

"Or it may be that I shall come to you again," she said, smiling bravely. "Here or beyond the stars, my beloved, in life or in death, I wait alone without you."

Bent called again, and I had to go. Looking back from the doorway of the room, I saw Eve standing with her arms outstretched as if to draw me back to her, and still she tried to smile till I should be gone.

We buckled on our revolvers and ammunition belts, but decided not to take our rifles—they were too conspicuous. At the entrance to the mansion an escort of six spearmen, sent by Ag, waited to precede us to the palace, more as escort than as guard, for they marched in pairs before us. Watkins pointed to their uniforms of fairly dark blue linen.

"If we'd gone to heaven instead of coming here," he remarked, "we'd have found Peter backed up on the gate by a squad of police in the same old blue. I do detest this lack of originality."

For my part, I remembered Ag's words about saving us all, spoken to me the night before, but in spite of them I knew that we might be nearer that squad of heavenly policemen than the length of a normal life. But there was nothing for it but to take such medicine as fate chose to administer, and, as unconcernedly as if it were merely an appearance in respect of unpaid income tax, we followed our escort toward the palace. We passed between them when they ranked off, three a side, at the spacious entrance, and raised their spear heads before their faces in token of salute as we marched in. The six of them, in the arching vastness of that royal portal, were no more than ants trying to look impressive at the edges of a garden path, but they gave me a thought of the splendour that must have been in the days of Kirtas-Asen and his ten thousand slaves.

We marched in, and the nave of Canterbury cathedral is not more nobly proportioned nor more impressive than the central hall of the king's palace in Kir-Asa—and Canterbury was built, while this was hewn. Two great rows of pillars went up to the arching roof in splendid fluted symmetry, spreading at their tops to carven designs; at the far end was the only glazed window we saw in the city, to these people the greatest treasure of their land, a thing beyond all price. Thick as was the glass, a pane here and there had been broken in the course of ages, but the fragments had been carefully gathered up and reset in such metal framing as one sees in old-fashioned casement windows. By the pale tints remaining in the glass, I judged that this window had once been brilliantly coloured, but that the hues had faded out during the centuries of its existence.

There were perhaps a couple of hundred people lost in the vastness of the hall, midway up which was set one of the great stone tables of the country, with, at its farther end, a great stone chair or throne that faced toward the door. On either side of the throne were two more stone chairs, not quite so sumptuous in their carving nor so high in the seats, and at the right-hand side of the table stood a group of a dozen blue-clad spearmen; I guessed that these last were intended to form a sort of ceremonial guard about us for the trial. We three stalked up with all the dignity at our command to the great stone table and there waited, facing the onlookers. Our footsteps wakened a resonance of echoes that took a long time to die out among the arches of the roof above us.

I had just time to take stock of those onlookers, and to observe that there were no women among them, before Ag, Neray, and three others who were evidently the remaining lords of the council entered through a doorway on the left of the hall. Ag came to us and greeted us in friendly fashion, but made no move to introduce us to our judges—Neray and the other three stood by the four chairs on either side of the throne. Standing by us, Ag looked at the spectators present. I saw him frown and shake his head.

"It is forbidden," he muttered angrily. "They know it is forbidden."

"What is forbidden?" I asked, trying to see the cause of his annoyance.

"See there, the three who stand bearing spears. He on the right is Comin-Saya, the king's heir. Next to him is Manos, and Macer stands on the left. It is forbidden that any man save the guards shall bear arms in this hall at a meeting of the council."

For this race, the three brothers were undersized men; Comin-Saya was shortest, and Macer tallest. The face of Comin-Saya was piggish, with little deep-set eyes; Manos looked an intellectual and moral degenerate, and Macer had a face of foxy cunning—of the three, I judged him cleverest and most to be feared. While I observed them, they came forward to within a little distance of the lower end of the council table.

"Ner Ag?" Comin-Saya called, in a high, thin voice, "rumour has come to me that the daughter I demand of you for wife is betrothed to a wandering stranger in our land. Speaks rumour truly, Ner-Ag?"

"Comin-Saya," Ag answered, "I bear with you and your brethren, being now your lord, as when you are king you in turn must bear with me and with the people of my house. Yet how is it that you, who some day must decree and proclaim the law, now break the law, bearing arms in the hall of the council?"

"It was our will to bear them," Manos the second brother growled, in a tone as far below the normal as was his brother's above it.

Comin-Saya bade him be silent, and took up the argument. "Ner-Ag," he piped, "I demand of you your daughter while she is yet free to consent, before the time is when I can take her unconsenting. I would have a willing bride."

"Were she free to consent, still would I give you no answer while you stand armed in the hall of council," Ag thrust back at him—and there was no small courage in this defiance of the man who would one day, and that perhaps very near, hold power of life and death over both Ag and Eve his daughter. "Put down your spears, you and your brothers, wait the end of the council's sitting, and then unarmed bring forward your requests, as is the right of all subjects of the council

97

which sits in the absence of the king."

I saw Comin-Saya half raise his spear, and his little eyes twinkled with rage—I could well believe that insanity was hereditary in his family, seeing him as he was then. He took a step forward, beyond his brothers.

"Say not that rumour speaks truly, Ner-Ag, for I will tear that daughter of yours from any man's arms when my day comes."

"Peace!" Ag thundered at him, and the echoes of the word rolled round the hall. "Disarm, before you are dragged before the council to answer for your words! My daughter is beyond your power, betrothed to this my guest. To that matter there is end, since the law shields her from even the king's claim. Now put down your arms and come up for judgment of the council, before you go back to your wine cups!"

Macer smiled evilly, but the face of Manos worked with rage at these bold words, and Comin-Saya slavered in utter fury—he was near on the madness that held his father from ruling, I saw. Suddenly he raised the spear he held and hurled it at us.

As one may watch a glass fall and yet be unable to arrest its splintering on the floor, so was I able to follow the spear through the score yards of its flight. Whether by accident or by design of the thrower, the blade twirled in the air as the weapon flew, and as it neared us I jerked back my head just in time. Blade and haft hissed past my face, almost touching me, and the point took Bent between the eyes, cleaving his skull so that he crumpled to the floor without a sound. In reality, a second sufficed to turn argument to tragedy, though to me the time between the casting of the spear and Bent's fall was long drawn out.

He had not fallen before the report of Watkins' revolver crashed and thundered with terrific suddenness through the great hall, and then my own weapon—I have no recollection of drawing it from its holster, and the movement must have been instinctive—set a second volley of deafening echoes rolling round and above us. Watkins' shot took Comin-Saya between the eyes, and mine hit Manos, who had raised his spear and stood poised in the act of throwing, in the breast. Comin-Saya fell dead as quietly as Bent had fallen, but Manos spun round, dropped to his knees, eased himself to proneness by his arms, and voiced his protest at so sudden an end with a moan that ended in a shuddering sigh. Thus beside the body of his brother he died, and I felt a little, fearful thrill at the death of this first man to fall by my hand.

Macer, the youngest brother of the three, who had watched and made no move, dropped his spear clattering on the rock floor and fled out through the great portal of the hall. The spectators would have followed after a brief interval of frozen terror at the roaring death and sight of the curling smoke from the pistol muzzles, but Watkins' voice pealed high and clear as they began to move.

"Halt!" he called, "or die as these have died!" and they halted where they stood. The four members of the council leaned aghast and trembling on their chairs, and even Ag, who knew us for his friends, looked fearfully at us, lords, as it seemed to him, of life and death.

"People of Kir-Asa," Watkins called again, "you have seen our power. These sons of a madman smote unawares, and of us killed one. For that one life we have taken two, and if again a hand should be raised against us we will take not two but twenty, except that the hand raised against us be a just hand, acting by the law. In proof of this we three, two living and one dead, are here to be judged of the council in that matter of which we are accused."

It was a subtle touch of his, that of submitting to justice in spite of the possession of such power as these people had never seen before. Now Ag, recovering from his fright as soon as any, bade the guards bear out the bodies of the king's sons, and also take away Bent's body to a separate chamber of the palace to await cremation. But before this last was done I knelt beside Bent and stripped off him the revolver belt—the heavy spear had driven right through the skull, its point protruding an inch or more behind. Watkins and I gave the limp hand a farewell grip apiece before they took him away; he had come through much with us, and we both remembered his premonition regarding the evil that Kir-Asa would bring him. He had fought the premonition, and how hard the fight had been we could not tell; thus we bade good-bye to our companion—companion no more.

Ag roused himself and the members of the council to their task, for which, after this exhibition of the power that we held, they had small liking. He took his place on the central throne while yet the blue-clad guards mopped up the blood of the king's sons from the floor; but, before he could speak to open the trial, footsteps came pattering from the door through which Ag himself had entered the hall, and an old, white-bearded man took his stand at the lower end of the great rock table.

"My lords of the council," he cried, "Saya-Comin the king is dead."

And, having given his message, he went back the way he had come. Ag made a little, impatient gesture, as if events crowded on him too swiftly, and he did not like it.

"Let us take our tasks in order, for they are heavy," he said. "First are we gathered to judge these strangers for the slaying of the Nantia, but judgment is now of no avail. For he who slew the Nantia lies slain by Comin-Saya the king's son, and these two his accessories have no rights in this our land. Thus how shall we doom the slayer, who is already dead, to death, or deprive his accessories to the slaying, who have no rights, of their rights? If that matter be ended, stand, members of the council, in token that it is passed."

The four rose to their feet as one, and as one sat down again—Ag's statement of the case and his conclusion were unanswerable. Ag looked from his throne toward us two. "Philip son of Wat Kins and Jack son of Faulk, by the order of the council are you now free. Let the use of your magic be tempered by the justice of the council."

"Set them not free yet," said Neray, "for there is yet another matter, Ner-Ag. By their magic they take for one life the lives of two men, yet since both those men bore arms in the hall of council, and sought to take the lives of the strangers, it may be that they were not to blame. Yet, if Saya-Comin the king died before Comin-Saya his son threw the spear, then is Philip son of Wat Kins slayer of Comin-Saya who at his father's death was king, though he reigned but for a minute.

And then, Comin-Saya being dead, Manos his brother was king, so that Jack son of Faulk is likewise slayer of a king. Now in the hands of the king is power of life and death—Comin-Saya being king by the death of his father, none may dream of vengeance on him should he decree death or with his own hand slay. So runs the law, Ner-Ag. Have these strangers taken just vengeance on the subjects of the council, or have they each slain a king?"

"Put like a lawyer," Watkins muttered to me, and I saw the quandry in which Ag was placed. If the king had died before his sons, then were we two subject to doom more surely than for the killing of the monkey woman, for the person of the king was sacred to an even greater degree than was that of the Nantia, and Ag, as head of the council, dare not attempt to protect us if we had each killed a king, as Neray put it. His position demanded that he deal out strict justice, and this even more now that the succession to the throne was made matter for question by Macer's flight from the hall.

I saw by his face that he thought swiftly. He might have put this matter off awhile, tried to gain time, but he elected to risk a chance.

"Stand, strangers, not yet being free, and since we would judge this matter with justice refrain from your magic," he bade. "Let a guard be sent to bring here the messenger who brought news of the king's death, and the physicians who were with him when he died."

A blue-clad guard went instantly, and we waited. "He's gambling on time," Watkins said to me, "and I admire the way he takes the risk. Anyhow, we have five chambers apiece left without reloading, and Bent's revolver hasn't been fired, while apart from the guards there isn't another weapon in the place."

"As prisoners, wait silently," Ag bade, and we spoke no more.

Four men came into the council hall through the door by which Ag had entered—evidently it led directly to the state apartments of the palace. They came, all old and bearded men, to the foot of the council table, and there waited to learn their errand.

"Let him who among you best knows tell us the manner of King Saya-Comin's death," Ag commanded.

101

The four consulted among themselves, and finally the one who had come as messenger and announced the king's death took upon himself to speak—we two took a grip on ourselves, knowing that our fate hung on the next few minutes, and prepared to play our game out either way.

"Lords of the council," said the old man, "Saya-Comin the king raved about his chamber until he fell as one exhausted, and we took him up and placed him on his bed, where he lay and breathed heavily for awhile. Then there came a great crashing noise as of thunder, and after that another noise like to the first. Thereat Saya-Comin the king rose upon his bed, and cried out: 'My sons—Alas, my sons!' as one who mourned. And with the words he fell back, so dying."

"It is enough," said Ag, "we need no more word than this." And the four old men returned whence they had come.

"My lords," Ag said, when the witnesses had gone.

"Saya-Comin lived to hear the thunder that slew Comin-Saya, and the thunder by which Manos died. Not for the space in which I speak these words, not for the time of one swift-taken breath, was either brother king, and these strangers slew men, subjects of the council that sits in the absence of the king, and who against all law bore arms in the hall of the council, seeking to compass their deaths. Say now, is there aught against the strangers?"

No voice answered him, but I saw Neray look vindictively at me, as if he would have found something against me if he could.

"Stand," Ag bade again, "if you agree my decision, that the strangers now go free."

As one the four stood and reseated themselves again, and, with precisely the formula and exhortation he had used before, again Ag told us that we were free. But we did not go.

"The fun is just going to begin, now," Watkins said to me, "and I think I'll take a hand in the plucking of this particular crow."

COUP D'ETAT

I stepped back to where the blue-clad spearmen stood grouped—so swiftly and unceremoniously had events swept on the assembly here that the formality of guarding us had not been observed—and was amused to see how they all recoiled from me as I moved. The memory of the vengeance we had taken on the king's sons was fresh on them, and they had no wish to get close to us. But I bade them have no fear, for I had need of a man from among them. One stepped out at the bidding of their chief.

"Go to the house of Ner-Ag," I ordered. "Seek out Eve, daughter of Ner-Ag, and tell her that Jack, son of Faulk, is unharmed and free."

He went unquestioningly. We might have bidden any man there pull out the great window of the council hall that day, and won obedience. And this message I had longed to send, from the moment Ag's judgment was spoken. I could picture Eve waiting hungrily, as I should have waited had the danger been hers, every minute an age, every passing foot-step a torture of disappointment. Hence I was glad to see that blue-clad back disappearing in the vastness of the entrance.

This done, I turned to see deadlock in the council. Had Comin-Saya been alive, there had been no council by this time. Had Macer not fled, not only would there have been no council, but Ag, Watkins, and myself had been in sorry case, probably awaiting execution (except that Watkins and I had our revolvers as arguments against such a settlement) for having killed the king's brothers, since Macer as king would hold power of life and death.

Now by the strict letter of the law, Macer was king, in spite of his flight. Equally past question, if Ag acknowledged Macer's kingship, he virtually signed his own death warrant, to say nothing of ours. The four remaining lords of the council, bound by the form of the law even more than Ag, were in a quandary. They wanted to acknowledge Macer as king, in accordance with the law, but between them and such a course stood—or rather sat—Ag, still possessed of more power than any one of them by virtue of his position, and backed by our terrible power, of which a most forcible example had been given to all present.

Watkins was right—the climax of the day's doings

was to come. Ag, who would probably have submitted to the decrees of fate and Macer had he been left to his own devices, had had a way of escape shown him. By Eve's betrothal to me he had tried to avoid that way, but now he was driven to taking it—he had no choice, except the unthinkable choice of recalling and submitting to the wrath of Macer. And, for his own safety, to get the full effect of the blow he must strike at once, before Macer could get in a word to anyone who held power in the land. Here, for the present, were concentrated the heads of power, and here must Ag make his stand. Watching him while the council sat in silence, and the spectators divided their attention between us two standing alone by the table and the five seated lords, I could tell from his face when he had made up his mind.

He stood, a noble figure of a man, to proclaim his will, and for a few seconds his gaze rested on us two, as if he would bespeak our aid.

"Guests of our country, lords of the council, and men of Kir-Asa," he began, "the council of five is dissolved, for King Saya-Comin, in whose name the council ruled, is dead. Thus I, Ner-Ag, head of the council, proclaim its dissolution as its last decree.

"Yet there is no king. Comin-Saya is dead, Manos is dead, and Macer as subject has broken the law and fled from the justice of the council. Shall he who so lightly holds the laws of the land rule over us, lords and people of Kir-Asa?"

He paused, and a buzz of amazed questionings began and grew among the spectators, while the four lords of the council stared at each other. It was not that they questioned the reasoning of his words, but law and custom held them so firmly bound that to question the authority of the royal house was a thing past their imagining; that Ner-Ag, the greatest man in the country under the king, should asperse royalty was a thing incredible.

"Two generations of the house of Saya-Comin have, by their madness, made need for a council to rule their stead," Ag went on, and the murmuring of voices in the hall ceased as he spoke. "The land is in the hands of its lords, not in the hands of its king, for half the time of a reign and more. Lords of the council, shall this thing be again? Will you"—and by quoting Watkins he proved how deeply that tempter's words had bitten in—"be slaves to a custom, submitting yourselves to a race that breeds madmen generation by generation, giving them power of life and death over you and your sons and daughters, or will you set up a king who shall deal justly, walk among you as one competent to rule, hold to the laws and in royal truth command the people of the land? Choose, and your choice is between a whip to lash your backs and a hand to aid serf and lord alike at need."

Such a straight appeal to reason, one would imagine, should have won a single, instant reply, but there came no reply at all. The two hundred or more who had come to witness our trial waited a lead, if they had an opinion on the subject. The lords of the council sat hesitating, and perhaps each of them wondering if he were the strong man competent to rule, to whom Ag referred. I had a strong suspicion that when, by implication, Ag referred to Macer as "a whip to lash your backs," he was not innocent of a tender regard for his own shoulder blades, but that was only natural.

He stood, having said his say, and the silence that followed was not unlike the uncomfortable pause that follows after a joke has fallen flat—there was a similar lack of response to the appeal to enthusiasm, and the situation was perilously near anti-climax when Watkins saved it. He counted on dramatic effect to win response; with a disgusted ejaculation of "Sheep!" he made one leap, and stood on the council table; there he stretched a pointing figure at Ag, standing before the throne, and cried out in the best melodramatic style:

"Lords of the council, rise! There stands your king!"

They came on their feet like automata when the conjurer pulls the string, and as for the people in the hall, what was good enough for the lords of the council was not for them to question. There were beads of perspiration on Ag's brow when the terrible suspense ended for him, and he sat back in the throne with an audible sigh of relief.

Still striking on hot iron, Watkins leaped down again from the table, marched to its end and bowed before the occupant of the throne of Kir-Asa. "O king," he said, "reign over this people justly and in peace, you and your house for ever. These lords of the provinces, standing here beside you, wait to declare their loyalty to your rule."

His back was toward me, and I wondered if he had his tongue in his cheek as he flung out this more than hint to the four lords. For my part, I thought it the most appaling impudence, from the point of view of these people, that he, an unknown stranger, should take the direction of their affairs into his own hands like this. By causing the four lords to declare their allegiance to Ag in presence of a couple of hundred witnesses, he would blaze the news all over Kir-Asa and the country beyond that Ag was supported by the representatives of all the power there was—he would commit these lords to a definite course and so wreck Macer's chance of winning adherents anywhere. It was sound policy, from Ag's point of view, but it was a daring, an impudent thing for Watkins to do.

Yet the colossal impudence of it helped in winning the desired effect. Those two revolver shots and their result went far to add weight to Watkins' suggestion, and the inexorable, relentless logic of the situation had weight too. The position was without precedent; had Macer returned, for all these lords knew a third clap of thunder might have reunited him to his brothers—and would that it had been so! Meanwhile, here sat their best man, claiming kingship, or in any case suggesting it, with his case backed by beings who threatened to take twenty lives for an attempt on one, and seemed capable of enforcing their threat.

The four lords were not anxious to declare their allegiance, but they did it. At a silent, slight gesture from Watkins, he who was evidently the oldest of them came before the throne, bowed before Ag, dropped on one knee, and with upraised hand promised to "hold my lands in trust and subject to the will of Ner-Ag, king, whom I acknowledge as given power of life and death throughout the land, and whose commands I obey at all times and in every place." It was a formula, and there was more of it; these words I remember.

Last, as youngest of the four, came Neray, and spoke the prescribed words. It irked him to say them, I saw, for Eve had been removed beyond his reach, and he could not forgive Ag's consent to the removal. His feeling was natural, I had to own. I was a stranger, an outsider whom nobody knew, while he was a fifth of the power of the land; the slight to him was not small.

Yet he promised. Then, mindful of the need for dramatic effect with such a people, Watkins turned to the watching throng, who had edged nearer, deeply interested in this—to them—epoch-marking series of events. In effect it was a revolution, yet never was a revolution so easily accomplished.

"Have you no word of welcome for your king, Ner-Ag?" Watkins called.

He struck the right note; Ag was well liked, and the roar of welcome that went up at his question was marred by no dissentient voice. The three provincial lords joined in, and Neray had another cause for grudge against me for he saw that I noted his silence.

There ensued a pause. I thought of Eve, waiting, wondering.

"Lords and people of Kir-Asa" the new king's voice fell on our ears, "this first day of my reign wears on'. Let messengers be sent forth bearing to all people my first decree: the time of sowing is past; the time of harvest is yet to come. Let there be three days of rest from labour throughout the land, beginning at dawn of the second day from now, that all men may honour this occasion as shall please them best.

"And my second decree: for the fourth part of the day that falls before noon, each day will I sit to hear the request of any man who shall come before me, lawfully and bearing no arms, in this my royal justice hall. And if any cause should prevent my thus sitting, one shall sit here in my place, as I for the time decree.

"So I, Ner-Ag, decree. Go forth."

"Good man," said Watkins to me. "I wondered if he'd know how to drop the curtain at the end of the act."

Neray, going out, passed us, and as he went he murmured a sentence of Ag's first decree——"The time of sowing is past, the time of harvest is yet to come."

Watkins looked after him. "My friend," he soliloquised, "I'm perfectly certain you're still qualifying for that thick ear, and you'll get it, yet."

Ag let Neray go, but bade friendly good-byes to the three provincial lords, telling them that he desired them to remain in the city for the next few days, and to confer with him here each morning. Since Neray's place was in the city his presence could be commanded at any time. It was evident that Ag had foreseen and thought out the possibilities of royalty since Watkins' first put the thought into his mind—those two decrees were too apt to the occasion to be spontaneous.

There remained with Ag and us two in the council hall some thirty spearmen, who ranged themselves in two lines between us and the doorway, and stood with their spears held at the salute, the broad blades almost hiding their faces. The spectators had all gone out at Ag's command. We passed between the two lines of guards, and when they had fallen in to follow us as escort, I ventured a question.

"King," I said, "how knew you that it was Ce Cil son of Bent who slew the Nantia?"

Ag looked at me with twinkling eyes. "I did not know," he answered, "but in causing it to be thought I freed you two of further charge in the matter."

So that was that. We went down the avenue to Ag's house, and he paused to dismiss our escort at the entrance. Then looking into the central hall of the house, he sighed a little. It looked homely and familiar after the bare splendour of the great royal hall.

"This was my home," Ag said. "Will that palace be home for me?"

It was a natural thought, but another thought held my mind from dwelling on it with him. I gave way for him to enter and pass straight up the hall, while for my part I turned and passed through a doorway that I knew to where one was waiting—oh, so eagerly and so patiently! For minutes there was no word between us, and I knew to the full the wisdom of the one who said that we should measure time by heart-beats, not by years. In time, hours had passed since Eve stood with arms outstretched to watch my going, but the hours were no measure of her waiting, nor of the great changes that had come about before her arms closed about me now and she gave willing lips to meet my own. For me had been the thrill of swift and fateful action, for her the woman's unseeing part.

I recall the light and shadow and light again on her face as I told her how the day had gone. Bent's death—in this my happiness I gave thought to him, so far as might be—Saya-Comin's death, the end of his two sons, the judgment of the council, Ag's kingship; Eve listened bewildered at the kaleidoscopic whirl that flung men about like puppets and turned her world upside down.

"You went prisoners for trial—you return friends of the king," she said wonderingly.

"True, Princess Eve," I answered, "and his daughter's very loyal subject bows before you."

"Nay," she said gravely, "for I am subject to my lord, to whom I have given my love, to whom at his word I give myself. Not even in jest speak thus, until——"

She ended the sentence by hiding her face on my breast, causing another silence that for awhile I dared not break, because of the hunger her unfinished sentence gave. At last she looked up at me again.

"Speak as you will, beloved," she said, "lest I think myself back in the time just past, questioning if ever your voice would gladden me again. But first—this for the messenger you sent to me to ease the time of waiting."

"This" was the first kiss she had given me unsought, and of her own will. I set down these things, little to others, perhaps, but never little to me, who loved her.

"Eve, my princess," I said after, "if I were impatient, eager to take you at your word——"

"Tell me," she bade, as I paused.

" 'To whom at his word I give myself,' you said," I reminded her. "One son of Saya-Comin has gone out free—there may be days of storm before us. If we faced them side by side. . . ."

For a little time she gazed at me; the colour deepened in her face, and her glorious eyes grew misty. Then slowly, and the surrender of the movement was infinite—she laid her head down on my shoulder, hiding her face. Her words were old as the world, new as to-day's dawn, wonderful as spring:

"Beloved," she said, "I have given you all my heart—I would slip into the shelter of your arms, to rest."

109

Before we sat to eat, Ag stood in his place before the table and spoke:

"My guests," he said, "my debt to you is greater than my power of payment. But for your wit and power I had been to-day helpless in the hands of Comin-Saya, whose will and worth you learned in the hall of council. You shall ask of the king, your friend, and no one thing that is justly in my power shall be denied you. I grieve for the empty place at this table, at which to-morrow we shall no more gather, and for a space hold silence that Ce Cil son of Bent may know that we keep him in memory, now that he looks down on us from beyond the stars."

After the silence that he asked, we sat down, a thoughtful party. The old order of things had passed. Ag, thinking that he must leave his home to go to the house of the kings, indicated the magnitude of the change that had come about. I wondered, but did not question yet, what chance Macer would have if he attempted reaction, and I remembered Neray and his allusion to sowing and the harvest to follow.

That night I questioned Ag; it had been decided that Bent's funeral should be held at the morrow's dawn, but there was one other matter on my mind. Ag gave me audience in the room in which he had sounded me with regard to betrothal to Eve.

"Speak freely, Jack son of Faulk," he bade. "Policy drove me to aid you but a day since, yet now the need for that policy has passed I am glad I gave the aid. Ask—I stand to give."

"I ask Eve," I said bluntly. "The times are stark—any day may see us out against Macer, out in defence of you, or even of ourselves—I put things before you at their worst. And this is Eve's will, as mine, that before any storm break on us we have right and your consent to face it together, as one."

"For my part," he answered, "I had rather waited till the storm passed and the sky cleared. Though in your haste is a measure of reason, recall that it is not eight days since you came strangers out of the west."

"Still I ask," I said, realising with difficulty that barely a fortnight had passed since we made the passage of the great chasm.

"And I give," Ag said with a smile, "for how shall I give to my kinsman or his friend to equal their gifts to me? When do you ask?"

"The second day from now," I said.

"Be it so," he agreed. "Jack, friend of my kinsman and friend to me, Ner-Ag, king, may this gift to you be valued at its worth, for it is a great gift."

"If need comes, and you seek our aid again," I said, "you shall see by my repayment if I value the gift."

Next morning we went out at dawn, up to the palace. Beside the stone table in the hall of the council stood a four-handled bier, on which lay that which had been Bent with its face uncovered, and as Ag, Watkins and I entered the hall four of the blue-clad spearmen took up the bier and with it marched out. An escort of sixty spearmen went with the bearers, and in utter silence we three followed.

From the time of our leaving the council hall no word was spoken until we reached our journey's end. We marched out from Kir-Asa at its eastern side, and an uphill road, half the width of the great avenue by which we had come to the city, took us a distance of about three miles to the foot of the volcano Kir. On either side, this avenue was bordered by masses of stone that had once been carved as alternate dinosauri and mastodons, but very few had kept enough of their original form to be recognisable. Here and there a gigantic, weather-worn neck reared up, or a trunk out-thrust at us as we passed. Then up the volcano's slope, which was easy of ascent, and the spearmen relieved each other in carrying the bier.

At the summit we descended a little way into the crater, only the bearers accompanying us, to a ledge of pumice rock which formed the last stage of this journey. Beneath us was twisting flame and pouring smoke, and on the rock on which we stood were marks where many such biers had rested. Here Watkins and I in turn came to look on Bent's face for the last time, and then Ag spoke the only words of the funeral rite:

"He who was has gone to stand before the lords of life and death—for this material shape he has no more need."

The four men lifted the bier and placed it at a point

111

where the rocky ledge inclined steeply. A slight push, and bier and body went down to vanish beneath the smoke-curtain that hid the volcano's heart. Then in silence we three returned.

Short as it was, the ritual comprehended all the facts of man's relations to time and eternity.

REVERIE

Of Eve I saw little before sunset of that day, for on her and on Niala devolved most of the business of transferring Ag's establishment to the house of the kings, as the royal palace was most commonly called. Ag himself, who had spared time to come with us for the committal of Bent's body to the flames of Kir, was busied with the three provincial lords until late, settling the redistribution of power consequent on his kingship, and so Watkins and I were left to consider our own selves and futures.

At least, though nominally we were out sight-seeing again, that was the main use to which we put the time. Watkins began by wanting to know what were my plans, in view of my forming the definite tie with Eve. I had to confess that I had no plans.

"I thought not," he said. "Jump at the one thing you want, and damn the cost. Well, it's natural, but think for a minute, Faulkner—do you mean to spend the rest of your life in this country?"

"Certainly not," I retorted. "I mean to take Eve, and go—she's willing, for we've talked it out."

"You would," he commented drily. "There's the danger of her missing her people, and wanting to come back, but it's no use considering that now. By the way, are you thinking of taking her the way of the chasm?"

"Impossible—we must find another way out."

"Quite impossible," he agreed. "No woman—not even your Eve—would face the ghosts of the valley—I'll tell you all about that, some time. For the present, I'll tell you my idea of what we ought to do."

We had climbed, by way of an interior stair that we discovered in a deserted mansion, to the flat rock roof, and looking out, could see in all directions across the country.

"First of all, now that we can get an idea of the lie of the land from here, tell me what are the ways out," I asked. For I had an idea that he would have learned these, and heaven knows what else, from Ag and Ner, while I had been otherwise engaged with Eve.

He pointed across the country in the direction from which we had come. "Consider the kingdom as an oblong," he said, "for it is that, nearly, and so small as easily to escape notice until this part of the country is properly surveyed and mapped—which won't be for many years, unless news of that gold store-house gets out and spreads. That side we came from is hedged by the gorge, and the way of the trembling bridge is the only way of crossing—you can get down, away there to the left, but not up again. The further cliff is sheer, though lower than where we crossed, and that infernal hot river has run close to it and burrowed an overhang of the rock."

"So much for that," I said. "What about the north?"

"Impassable jungle, with tree-trunks feet deep in water, nearly all the length of the north side," he said, "and morass right up the rest of the way to where the country dries up and the hills begin—this volcano is a spur from the range. But there's hard rock this side the jungle, and a river that comes round from the back of the volcano as we're standing flows to that hard rock. The land on that side used to be the bed of a big lake occupying what is now the north of the country, but somebody, probably the people who planned this city, cut a sloping gully twenty feet wide in the rock to drain the lake. The river goes down that gully like a mill-race for nearly a mile, and then loses itself to form the morass. That gully of the river makes a second way out of the country, but nobody could ever come in by it. You get to morass, abandon your boat and take your chance. With your Eve, it's the only way out."

"This way?" I asked, pointing to the volcano, set in the third side of the oblong.

Watkins shook his head. "When you get over the river, waterless hills and valleys—like that valley we came down," he answered. "Nobody here knows, but I know from the map it drops to blank jungle—I can remember the conformation so far. You'd probably be dead of thirst before you reached that jungle."

"And south?" I took his word as to the impossibility of the way beyond the volcano.

"Hills and no water for about four days' journey, and what Ag calls poison-dart people swarm beyond—by the way, their villages run up to within a few miles of where we crossed the gorge. The desert stretch is wide enough to keep them out, and where they can't cross that sort of country we needn't attempt it."

I knew enough to refrain from questioning this, and in any case had no mind to venture into country where the natives used poisoned arrows, either with or without Eve.

"And now your plans," I said.

"Good old Faulkner!" Watkins exclaimed. "Still sticking to the terms of the bargain, in spite of your Eve. Well, I'm in no hurry to leave. It's no small thing to plant a king on a throne, and now I mean to stay long enough to solder him down on it. He's a sort of relative of mine—it's for the good of the Watkins family."

I let that pass—he could account for his whims how he liked.

"I've discussed it with Ag, and he's grateful," he went on. "For the present we can only wait—things look quiet, but Ag agrees with me that Macer isn't coming in to kow-tow without putting up a fight. His people have been kings from the beginning of time, or longer, and he'll do his damndest to be king too. I don't mean to let him."

"What are the chances of fighting?" I asked.

Watkins laughed. "There hasn't been a fight in the country since the legendary period," he said, "for there's been no cause. They're a peaceful people by instinct, and they haven't to defend themselves against invasion—the monkey woman and her guard do all that, and in a good, fertile country a small population won't fight among themselves—unless they're Irish. They simply don't know how to begin to fight."

"But these guards—they're armed," I suggested.

He made a gesture of derision. "Two hundred of them all told in the city," he said. "They can throw their spears and stab at close quarters—there's absolutely no other form of weapon surviving, unless you count the knives they use for their food, and as far as I can make out there are no paintings or carvings anywhere that would give the race an idea, except for that heraldic device of the axe on Kirtas-Asen's tablet of gold. They face wild animals with nothing more than these spears, on the borders of the country."

"Let's go down," I said, for the afternoon was drawing on. We went down through the empty mansion into the street, and made our way back toward the palace.

"What force could Macer raise, at the utmost?" I asked as we went.

"With the men on the lands belonging to the king—if he can get their adherence—about eight hundred, altogether," Watkins answered, "but Ag doesn't know if he can find spears for all of them. And since it has never been tried, there's no telling whether they'd fight for toffee. I've told Ag to keep every smith in Kir-Asa working overtime forging spears."

"And shields?" I asked.

He swore beautifully at his own oversight. "Never thought of them," he confessed. "One for you, Faulkner. I'll get out a design and make 'em get busy on shields—it'll be one in the eye for Macer if he gets up and kicks."

"As he will," I prophesied.

"A few rifle bullets, and Ag is settled in his place, so long as one of the bullets gets Macer—his half-mad race is best exterminated, anyhow. A people like this can't afford degenerates, any more than it can afford wars."

"Isn't there collateral stock?" I asked.

Watkins shook his head. "Their record appears to have been one son for generations, till the last king broke all records for the country by having three. Macer is the only surviving claimant."

"And with any luck we'll settle his claim before we go," I said.

When we were nearing the palace Watkins suddenly stopped in the street.

"Here, before we go in, Faulkner," he said, "I want to make you a wedding present. To-morrow you get your heart's desire, and I want, if possible, to give you the next three days clear with Eve, whatever we have to stand against later. I'll keep close touch with Ag, and call on you if there's any need—I want you to feel that you need worry about nothing at all, for just as long as I can give you, and the three days sure. Ag is handing over his mansion to you, with a paltry forty servants to clean your boots and bring your shaving water—my gift is the three clear days."

I could not answer, save for a hand-grip that he understood. There was a kindly smile on his good, ugly face as we paused there. But a few weeks ago we had made a mere business bargain over coming on this venture; now, I knew, I had made a friend for life.

"Faulkner," he said, "I like your Eve. Three of us came as one, three will go as one—and I'll take the steering oar when we go down the rapids of the gully we haven't seen yet. For your three days, be as happy as if you were the first Eve's mate in the garden, and I'd wish you more if I could."

He set off again toward the palace without giving me a chance to thank him properly.

The six of us, Ag and his family, Watkins and I, spent that evening together in one of the lesser state apartments, on the opposite side of the council hall to that in which Saya-Comin and his sons had lived. Their swinish habits had rendered a thorough spring cleaning of their rooms imperative before Ag would think of using them—or before Niala would let him.

We were quietly content, and sat until late, Watkins and I learning more of the country's ways. Niala was first to go, and then Eve went with me beyond the door of the room, where I took her in my arms.

"To let you go for the last time," I told her.

"Lord of my heart, I, too, wait," she whispered, and so fled away from me. Then I went back, and Ag told me the nature of the simple ceremony of the morrow. Thus that day ended, and Watkins and I were conducted to a room in the palace to which our rifles and all our belongings had been brought from Ag's house.

"You can take your own personal necessities and make 'em up in a bundle," Watkins told me. "I'll see that they're sent back for you, so you don't have to bother about that."

"I ought to include one of the rifles," I said.

"No," Watkins disagreed. "I'll take care of all the stuff till we join forces again for serious work. You've got your revolver as defence in sudden need, and it's enough. When you want a rifle, you'll want me there with another one, and I shall be there. Now do as you're told, like a good little boy."

Of what passed the next day I retain detached mind-pictures, but no connected series of events such as would form definite record. There is a picture of the great hall of the council, filled, now, with people—for it was the first day of their holiday, and all were free to come. I recall Ag's and Watkins' faces—but no other face was clear—as they waited by the carven throne, and a long clear lane from where they stood to the great portal, between the watching people. I recall Eve, coming through the great doorway and up that lane quite alone—coming as she had come the night Ag sent her to me, neither hurrying nor faltering, but with a gracious dignity that I have never seen excelled. She wore over her richly embroidered linen robes a great mantle, of which the edges trailed on the ground; it was the finest woven tissue of pure gold, and was a legacy from the old race, for these people had not the art of such weaving nor that of drawing gold to such fine strands. She came straight to me, clasped her hands together and laid them in my own, and Ag's voice comes back to me as he said, "Now are these two one." And for me first, and then for Eve, remained to say, "Now are we two one." This said, the ceremony was ended.

A picture of a feast, at which we two sat side by side. Of speaking with the lords of the council and with others. Of Neray's face somewhere in the throng that eddied round us. Of Watkins, sober old Watkins, kissing Eve on the brow, speaking with her, and admiring that wonderful golden mantle, so fine as to be a transparency about her. Of her gay laughter with the mischievous note in it, as men and women came and went, and of Ag, grave and with some added dignity grown about him since we first stood with him in this council hall—he made a fitting king.

Of the throngs thinning, going. Of how at last we two left Ag, his wife and son, and Watkins, in the

117

arching vastness of the palace entrance, and with a
hundred guards about us went down the avenue, Eve
leaning on my arm; of the setting sun striking myriad
gleams from her robe of gold.

Of passing in to the hall of the mansion while our
guard stood at the salute. Of coming at last to a room
that before this hour I had not entered, and there
taking from my princess the shining golden robe, not
brighter now than the light from her eyes. Of her
unbound hair that made a curtain about her face. . . .

Thus, as she desired, she slipped into my arms to
rest.

I had meant to tell of the three days, Watkins' gift
to us, but the long minutes pass and no word comes. It
is in my heart, that perfection of world-forgetting, but
I find it not a thing that can be told. Here in this
record I have kept back nothing, so far, and it is not by
will that the tale of these days is withheld. It is that
they were past all telling wonderful.

The fresh beauty of English woodland in early
summer dawns; the perfection of the world's great love
songs, and their infinity of desire; the music that is in
the long, slow roll of waves on to a quiet shore; the
splendour of gold and flashing gems; the fragrance of
old gardens, and the questing sweetness that is in the
breath of the west wind come over harvest fields—like
these, and more than these, was Eve to me. To put that
perfect time into little words of mere description, to
attempt picturing it by statement of what we said or
where we passed it, would be banal and small, dust on
the mirror of a time that was out of time. If we spoke,
it was not that we needed speech, for we two were
one.

This I set down in place of the record I would have
made—set down with a touch of reverence for my
princess, again hearing her happy laughter of those
unthinking, perfect days. I have tried to tell of them,
and failed.

The great stone table had been moved aside in the
central hall, and a little table of carven hardwood—a
recessed block like the stone table—had been set in
place for us two, for Niala had thought for her

daughter as Watkins had thought for me. Here we sat, having eaten, on the morning of the fourth day, and here Watkins, entering, found us.

"Well," he said cheerily, speaking in the native tongue that Eve might not feel out of it, "we have left you to each other for as long as might be. And you?"

"Value your wedding gift as one to keep in mind while we live," I answered.

Eve smiled her concurrence. "And now it is over?" she half asserted and half questioned.

Watkins hesitated, as if reluctant to end things for us.

"We know nothing of what is going on about us," I said. "So good has your gift been to us both."

"And now we need you, Jack," he said, "both the king and I. Neray fled to Macer on your wedding night. We hold the city, and how much of the country we hold we cannot tell. I hope to have more spies in when I return to the palace, and meanwhile the smiths are still forging spears."

"Eve," I said, "we will go back to the palace. I could have wished this time not so short."

"And I," she said with a little sigh, though she smiled at Watkins. "Yet if all life were such as these perfect days have been, how should we be content to stand beyond the stars?"

It was a brave saying. She looked back at the empty hall as we went out, and I saw her lips quivering.

"Beloved," I said, "we go as we shall return, together."

And at that she smiled again.

CHALLENGE AND REPLY

Watkins came with us to the council hall in which Ag and the three lords of the provinces were gathered with certain administrative officials and minor dignitaries, who, following their masters, adhered to Ag. I took Eve through to Niala in the royal apartments, and left her there, myself returning to the council hall.

I was in time to see a commotion down by the entrance, out of which emerged four of the uniformed

119

spearmen and a woman who walked in their midst. The little group came up to the end of the council table, and, facing Ag on his throne, paused. I heard the three lords whisper among themselves as they stood grouped beside Ag, and looked from them to the woman, the cause of their whispering.

She was tall and slight, very fair-skinned, and, like Eve's, her hair was brown, not black—they two were the only exceptions in this matter that I saw among the women—I believe they were the only two in the kingdom. This woman was no older than Eve, and had been no less beautiful, but there was stamped on her face the expression of one who has sold her birthright among her people and been cheated of the price. Her grey robe was greyer for the dust of travel; her eyes were heavy with weariness, but apart from that one need hardly look to see that the woman had wept all her tears, and now went dry-eyed in an eternity of despair.

"Your name and place, woman?" Ag asked—though he knew.

"My name, Eina. I come messenger from Macer, king, to the lords who were of the council of Saya-Comin, king, and who still hold to Ag, thief of Macer's throne. Macer will send no man to be slain, knowing that a woman may speak and go free."

She spoke indifferently, though the daring insult of the words was doubled by the hint that Ag was capable of violating the sanctity of a herald, had that herald been a man. Days before, when we had talked with Ag, he had told us of this woman. She had been once a happy young wife to one of the head men of the king's lands; Macer had seen and desired her, and she had left husband and child to go to him, the king's son. In this land where the chastity of women was a thing of ten times more account than in civilised countries, her sin was one that no man nor woman could forgive, and by its great rarity was more than ten times as conspicuous. Ag looked his wrath at her bold words.

"On your knee, woman," he bade sternly; "deliver this message of a fled subject to your king and his."

The woman knelt without hesitation, as if it were all one to her how the message was spoken. "Lords," she said, "I am but a voice, nothing more. Hear the words

120

of the voice, then silence it if you will."

"Nay, Eina," said Ag more gently, "for I decree it as your punishment that you live and go free. From your face I read that I could speak no harsher sentence, no doom more terrible. Rise, being sentenced. Speak the words of Macer without fear."

She rose, but not so indifferently as she had knelt, for that sentence stung her beyond any harshness or threat of punishment. She spoke her message, as bidden:

"From Macer, king, to such of his subjects as hold to Ag, the thief, in forgetfulness of the law.

"I have gathered up the men of the king's lands and armed them for war, yet would I not war against my people, but only against Ag, son of Ner (the name, spoken in such form, was unforgiveable insult, conveying a slur on Ag's mother) to whom in their error they have given support. Thus, having gathered up my men, for the space of three days after this message is spoken I will hold my hand, that they may deliver up to me Ag and the people of Ag and the strangers who are with him, for my vengeance. Yet, having moved to the western border with my men, will I in that three days give the house of Ag to destruction by flame, as token of my power.

"If at the end of the three days Ag and his people and the strangers be not given up to me, with my men will I advance from the west. First will I lay waste the province Ag ruled, slaying every man and giving all the women to my men to use as they will. And if still my subjects in Kir-Asa will not give up Ag, so will I deal with each province in turn, saving only the king's lands. So shall there be no harvest, and the people that are in Kir-Asa shall starve.

"And if, when all the land is laid waste, save only the lands of the king: when all its men are slain, all its women spoil of my men—if then Ag and his people are not given up, then will I lead across the land the things of the waste, that its women may be destroyed and the kingdom, all but my people dwelling in the lands of the king, shall cease to be.

"But if Ag, and the people of Ag, and the strangers, be given up to me bound, there shall be pardon without question for all who in error have given support to Ag, and the land shall be at peace.

"Thus I, Macer, king, decree."

I could well understand that Eina, bearing such a message, looked for death at the end—though I did not then know the full terror embodied in Macer's decree. Yet I saw a look of definite fear on Ag's face when she spoke of the "things of the waste," though to me there was no special threat in this part of a message that was all threat. It was spoken monotonously, with just sufficient emphasis and inflexion to give every word its intended meaning, and no more, and, weary though the woman was, her voice was one of far more than normal sweetness.

"Woman," said Ag, "we have heard. Wait, and take back our answer when it is prepared."

Since the preparation was evident from the answer itself, there is no need to detail our conference. Ag, Watkins and I, and the three lords were chief framers, and we got a writer who inscribed four copies on thin wooden sheets covered with hard wax. Three of these copies Eina took with her, and one we kept; before she went, Ag also read the answer aloud, mainly to remove the effect of Macer's threats from the minds of those who had heard Eina speak. This was the answer:

"Ner-Ag, king, to such of his subjects as follow the unjudged fugitive from justice, Macer.

"For the space of ten days from the sending forth of this my message shall it be given to you to come to my royal council hall, and, laying down your arms, go free.

"I will make no war, I will slay no man, lay waste no home, and harm no woman, if this be done. But I will send forth my army under Philip my kinsman and Jack the son of Faulk with him, to destroy such as will not cease from following Macer, that my kingdom may remain unharmed from the western border to Kir-Asa, where I sit to rule. Such men as do not submit shall take the risk of their defiance, for my army shall come against them not only with spears, but with thunder and flame that blasts and slays as Saya-Comin's sons were slain in this my council hall. In battle is my army very terrible, but to such as surrender within the appointed time will I give peace.

"Though I would have judged and sentenced Macer rather in mercy than in strict justice, had he

122

surrendered himself to be judged by the law, yet since he has threatened to invoke and lead the things of the waste against the women of my kingdom, he is beyond mercy. Him, when taken, will I cause to be bound living and unharmed to such a bier as is used for the carrying of the royal dead. On the bier shall he be taken to the summit of Kir, the mountain of fire, and thence sent bound and living on the path of the bodies of the royal dead. Any such of my subjects as are taken with him, after the ten days grace are ended, shall follow him, bound and living, into the flame. Only the woman, Eina, should she be taken with him, shall go unharmed and free.

"Thus I, Ner-Ag, king, decree."

The woman heard, and spoke no word. Watkins handed her the light burden that she must take with her.

"I would ask," he said courteously, "that you be given food and drink here, and store to take with you on your journey. And I would ask, too, that of this message one writing shall be given to Neray, sometime governor of this city."

"To Neray will I give one," she answered. "Here will I neither eat nor drink, nor will I take any store, being Macer's woman and among Macer's enemies. Is it your will, lords, that I go?"

"Go, woman," Ag bade.

The guards stood back from beside her. She turned and went steadily the way she had come.

The decree allotted to us our places. Ag would remain at Kir-Asa, king of such subjects as remained loyal, while Watkins, generalissimo, took the four hundred or so of men who made up the total the city had raised—including the two hundred of the guard. The rest were volunteers, though there was a well-known law which gave power to the king to embody such of his subjects as he chose. We relied more on the terror of firearms, coupled with the probable effect of Ag's proclamation in causing desertions from Macer's party, than on numbers of spearmen. We were glad of enough men to make a show, and trusted that they would not run when confronted by superior numbers. To that end, in discussing the matter, we suggested mixing up the untrained men among the guards, though Watkins did not press the suggestion. The discipline of the guards, though slight, might have a steadying effect on the whole.

I went mainly because I doubled the firearm value of the force; for that reason—the moral effect of rifle and revolver fire, and of the shot gun, which we took as of value at close quarters—I had to go. We had a vague idea of training one of the chiefs of the guard to use Bent's revolver, but our supply of ammunition was too short, for one thing, and for another it would have spoilt our reputation for magic if we made him as potent as ourselves. This man, Tain by name, we reserved for another purpose.

We gave our men the day for preparation, so as to start on the following morning. It was too late, even if we set out at once, to prevent Macer from setting fire to Ag's homestead, and by starting on the morrow we should still be in the line of Macer's attack when he set out, at the end of his three days' grace, on his campaign for the destruction of the western province. There was the plan, beautiful in its simplicity; Watkins and I discussed it with Ag, with the chiefs of the administration, and with the three lords of the provinces whom Ag had held in Kir-Asa, so far. We caused this plan to be blazoned throughout all Kir-Asa as our intention. We almost shouted it in the streets, and let the men of the guard proclaim it where they would, taking them all into our confidence, that they might know what they had to do. We might as well have sent messengers to Macer, explaining the details of our campaign and furnishing him with a time-table, so as to save his spies, of whom we felt certain there would be some in Kir-Asa, the trouble of telling him the news.

That night, while Kir-Asa slept, we two told Ag our real plan—in spite of his entire ignorance of military affairs, he had been a little puzzled over our lack of reticence, up to then. I bade farewell to Eve, who would stay under her father's protection until we should return, and went with Watkins to the quarters of the guard. The volunteers, having no quarters allotted to them, slept at their homes, and were to muster before the palace in the morning. In half an hour, or less, we had the sleepy, wondering, two hundred guards on parade in their blue uniforms, all save Tain, who would take his orders from Ag himself in the morning. Ten minutes after forming we marched off from the open space before the palace, while Ag and Eve, standing in the shadows of the entrance, watched us go under the light of the young moon. Eve waved to me as we went, and I waved back at her. Not a man of our command, save for Watkins and myself, knew his destination.

"Nicely done," Watkins remarked to me in a satisfied way. "With half an hour's rest on the way, we'll be at the edge of the king's lands by dawn. By noon the royal country house ought to be well ablaze, and by nightfall nearly every man of the royal retainers ought to be scampering back from Macer to surrender and save his home and skin. Macer won't have a rag left."

"We mustn't be too certain," I remarked. "He knows what will happen when he's caught, or will as soon as Eina gets back to him, and he may retain some men."

"If Tain gets our two hundred volunteers on the march in the morning according to plan," Watkins said, "they ought to arrive on the western border just when Macer's survivals are sickest over the desertions. And that, by my calculations, will leave Macer as the solitary gold-fish in the bowl."

We marched out of the city, turned to the left off the great road when we had got down the incline to where fertile lands began, and called to the head of our force two of its members who knew the route to the royal domain, bidding them precede the force by a few yards as guides. Watkins and I dropped to the rear to see that no man fell out under any pretext, and for another two hours we tramped on steadily. We made our half-hour halt as arranged, marched on at its end, and again halted when the moon was just on setting, to wait for dawn. From the way our guides described the rest of the journey, another hour's march would bring us to what Macer regarded as his country house.

We marshalled our men into a stone-walled cattle-pen or enclosure, partly to keep them from being seen, and still more to assure ourselves against

125

the possibility of desertions—any man trying to get over the wall of the enclosure would show up against the sky, and the shotgun was loaded and ready as a hint to any second man who might think of following a possible first. We counted them into the pen, and found all present; once there, they stayed—our fears of desertion were groundless.

"And now we're settled down," Watkins said to me as we squatted in the entrance to the enclosure, "I want to explain to you the black devilry of Macer's threat about the 'things of the waste.' You may have thought Ag's sentence on Macer himself a bit harsh, but after that threat it wasn't harsh enough."

"The 'things of the waste' are the beings we met in the valley," I suggested.

"Quite right," he agreed. "I don't know if you felt, when they came near us, a sense of evil—of absolute hatefulness. I know I did."

"So did I," I said, recalling the feeling quite clearly, though the rush of subsequent events had driven it from my mind until he spoke.

"They are evil," he averred emphatically; "too evil to blend even with the Piltdown and Neanderthal brute-man types to make for intellectual progression—they are the dregs of human forming in the beginning of time, the useless evil that was left. Half-human and half-spirit as they are, they form the nearest approach to the popular conception of devils one can admit as existing—probably contact with them or something like them in very early historic times gave rise to the legends of demons and familiar spirits that have come down to us, and as they retreated to one or two waste places of the world, they have survived unseen."

"But if they can't 'blend,' as you put it, what harm can they do?" I asked.

"I'll tell you exactly what Ag told me," he answered. "There's no proof of it either way, for no woman has come in contact with them for centuries, though the surviving horror of them is so great that you mustn't speak of them before a woman. You saw that, with Niala and Eve."

"And couldn't understand it," I said.

"Neither could I, then. They can't harm a man, but

any woman with whom they come in contact, and any girl as well, right down to babyhood, either loses her reason or dies. So Ag believes, and though I myself don't think this possible in any supernatural way, yet the effect of their hateful presence might be enough to rob any woman of her reason, or kill her by shock. And here's one reason why these people have never got out from their country toward the coast; the only way that they had is impassable to their women, and though the men might cross the gorge they couldn't take their families and belongings with them, even supposing they had the colonising instinct."

"But how could Macer lead these things?" I asked.

"In spite of their lack of intellect, a man can—again this is according to Ag—place himself in sympathy with them, instil the one idea of easy prey into them, and then they'll follow him, even into peopled country, so long as he's there to lead. And with every victim—that is, with every woman or girl they meet—they gain strength and confidence."

"It's too horrible to be true," I said.

"Possibly," he answered. "I maintain an open mind on the subject. Who would have believed that a woman could control and direct a horde of fierce apes—and yet we know that to be true. In any case, Macer would only seek communion with the things of the waste, and support from them, in utter desperation. It would be the sort of pawning his soul that no man would contemplate while a ray of hope remained. Even when he hasn't a man beside him, still he'll hesitate."

"There's madness in his breed," I reminded him.

"Yes, but still . . ." he said, as if trying to convince himself. "Anyhow, we won't give him the chance. I had to get you to come with me to help hold these men together to-night, but as soon as the royal residence ahead of us is well alight you can take an escort of half-a-dozen men and get to the western border in time to stiffen up the volunteers with a little shooting. We should have Macer caught and on his way to the crater in about three days."

"I'd better shoot him, and save that horror," I said.

"Perhaps—and yet I don't know," Watkins answered reflectively. "The only horror about it is the anticipation, and Macer is too low a brute to feel that

127

overmuch—the actual death in the crater would be swift enough. And look at the moral effect. I spoke of soldering Ag on the throne, but carrying out a punishment like that would rivet him there."

"Supposing we catch our hare?" I suggested.

He laughed gently. "A reasonable idea," he agreed. "We are running past ourselves a bit. Look—there's dawn showing—in ten minutes we can begin to turn our men out."

MISHAPS

There were things in the royal country house which made our work of destruction a tragedy, from the viewpoint of the archaeologist. Here, and nowhere else in the country, we found what we took to be traces of the race that came after the Atlantean founders of Kir-Asa, and before the present occupants of the land—the intermediate race of which we had been told as occupying before the people we knew came, perhaps to conquer, and in any case to replace them. It is interesting to conjecture, that of how the first founders of Kir-Asa died out, how and whence the second race came, and then how this third nation ousted them in turn. How they came, whence they came, and the time of each occupation, must remain matter for conjecture.

The royal house was built of blocks of stone, irregular in shape, and set in a whitish cement which in places had softened until one could pick it away with the finger-nail. Within, we found that a partition between two of the rooms was of solid ivory, the sections being beautifully fitted to each other. Then there was a room panelled with dark wood, with an inlay of severe geometrical pattern in lighter colour, and the massive rafters under the planking to which the thatch was fixed were carved with gargoylish faces in high relief. We noted the contrast between this work and that in Ag's house, which showed the thatch laid on to bamboo rafters, without a plank lining to hide the reeds. Bare thatch on bamboo was the invariable rule with the present inhabitants; here was evidence of another order of things. And the whole place was a riot of wood and ivory carving, including the circular wooden doors—similar to the stone discs at the entrance to Kir-Asa—which rolled back into recesses in the wall to give entry both to the main hall and to the chambers of the interior.

It seemed that the first Atlantean occupants of the country, workers in stone and metal, had devoted their attention mainly to things of practical utility. If they had gone in for carving and beautifying their belongings, the vast lapse of time since they died out as a race had destroyed all traces, just as it had destroyed the colouring of the glass in the one surviving window we saw. This second race—assuming that all this work was theirs—was more inclined to decorative arts, and to beautifying all they had inherited from their predecessors. So we saw it; the founders of the country were a great people, the second an artistic race, and this third order a mere occupancy, adding nothing, but merely using what they found.

But these reflections came later—we had neither time to consider these things nor tools to deal with them, if we had wished to save evidences of the intermediate race, against which course there was a strong argument. We could only admire, and regret the need that drove us to a destruction which would render us the last admirers. First the remaining occupants of the place, mainly women and children, though a good number of men remained, were cleared out and rounded up under control of the guard so that they could see the fire. Then, acting under our instructions, a detachment of our men made piles of combustible furniture in two of the rooms, and Watkins lighted one while I attended to the other. It was the first time we had needed matches since our arrival, and as I struck a vesta on the sole of my boot, instead of indulging in the lengthy metal, stone and tinder process for producing fire, a big scared "O-oh!" went up from the few guards who watched.

We held the previous occupants of the place watching, until the boarding was a roaring furnace, its roof fallen in and its walls cracking, and then we withdrew the guards and let the people go in, the knowledge that one or more would go straight to Macer's force with tidings of the destruction which he had reserved from the general doom with which he threatened the rest of the country. Our men, unused as they were to this sort of work, obeyed commands implicitly, and I was glad to see that they evinced no inclination to loot or exceed their orders. They even worked actively in saving a group of reed huts from catching fire, keeping the huts nearest to the flaming palace damp by throwing water until all danger had passed.

I could grieve yet in recalling that burning of carven walls and rafters, hangings of cloth of gold and dainty furnishings, strange things of earthenware and wood adornment—the treasures of centuries heaped in one great dwelling, to go up in smoke in a puny quarrel like this! Watkins had a thought of saving some of the smaller things; small and large alike were not merely priceless, for the word is feeble to describe them, unmatched as they were, and without like in all the world.

"If you take a rag or a scrap," I said, "how will you stop these guards if they show signs of wanting to loot?"

"Quite right," he agreed. "As far as the guards are concerned, one shot would soon stop any looting, but if we are to make law we must be above breaking it—but look at that ivory cornice!"

So, reluctantly, we fired it all, and before it had burnt out—that is, well before noon—I set out with six men of the guard to link up with the volunteers from Kir-Asa near the western border and lead them against such men as Macer might have left. We had come some miles from the line of the great paved road, and the one of my men who best knew the way led us still further from the road at first, because of a river, swift-flowing and dangerous to swim, and too deep to ford, which flowed between us and the road. Having at last crossed this obstacle by a bridge farther down the stream, we were able to take a straight course across country for the western border.

We crossed this river on the second day, at a little after noon, and were then well into Ag's province of the west, not far from our journey's end. We had travelled swiftly, and I was nearly tired out. My rifle and the packets of ammunition for use with it had so far been carried in turns by my six men; I had the heavy revolver and its fifty rounds—or rather, the forty-nine remaining since I shot Manos—all the time. We carried each a ration of dried strips of meat that would last indefinitely, so as to be ready in case of emergency, but we lived on the country. It was necessary only to stop at any of the numerous groups of reed huts with which the land was dotted, and to ask; the people gave us all we needed. As Ag had told us, there was enough for all.

Down by the bridge by which we crossed the river, and on that river's far bank, a stone dwelling-house stood empty and without furnishings, though in perfect repair—as if its tenants had moved out yesterday, and new holders would come in on the morrow. The house itself was over-shadowed by several kinds of palm; between it and the river, on a rich stretch of lawn, half a dozen flowering trees blazed, crimson and gold, and there were plantain and great glossy-leaved shrubs—it was a little Eden of a place. Our guide, who came originally from this western province, told me the place was one of Ag's pleasure houses, furnished from his main residence when he chose to use it. Hence its perfect state of repair, and its present emptiness—it was long since Ag had been here, the guide said. Not since the last king's insanity called for the formation of the council, he thought.

My thought, as I lay down with a heap of fragrant dead leaves for a pillow, was that the place would make a perfect little retreat for Eve and me. I had it in mind to make another week or fortnight quite alone with her, when this business should be ended and before we left the country.

Before lying down, I took one of my men to a certain spot, and bade him observe one of the shorter of the palm trees. I explained carefully to him that, when the sun began to sink behind the palm as he stood on this spot, he must waken me. Then I lay down and almost instantly was dead asleep, for I was very weary.

The sun was high over that palm when I fell asleep. As it sank westward—and this I had overlooked in giving my man his instructions for wakening me—it described an arc in the sky, coming down to the side of the palm as one stood on the spot I had indicated to him. The bucolic fool, half through fear of wakening me when he ought not, and half through stupidity, waited for the sun to move across the sky and place itself over the top of the palm, apparently. In any case, it was half-way down the trunk of the tree, as one observed it from that particular spot where I had bidden the man stand, when I wakened of my own accord and sat up with a start realising how much of the day had gone.

Well, swearing was no good, and one could hardly hope, after all, to carry such a venture through without some minor mishaps—inwardly I prayed that this might be only a minor one. I took the rifle and ammunition myself, now, and we went on. Some way before us—perhaps three or four miles—opaque clouds of smoke blotted out the sunset, telling us that Macer had fired Ag's home, probably immediately on hearing of the burning we had carried out.

To either side of us, now, men fled eastward both singly and in scattered groups, the greater number being away on the side nearest to the great road. They steered wide of us as soon as they saw us approaching, and I judged them to be deserters from Macer's force, fleeing back toward their homes. At last, when we were nearing the burning house, and the sun was just touching the horizon, one came straight toward us. It was Tain, the chief of the guard whom we had left in Kir-Asa to lead the volunteers on their march, breathless, and carrying a spear. He knew us by the light, coming from behind him, falling on the blue uniforms of my six guardsmen. He did deep reverence before me, and stood silent, fearing to speak.

"Tell me what has passed, without fear," I bade.

"Lord," said Tain, "when it fell to these men to fight, every man save only myself hurled his second spear at a man of Macer's. Then were they all weaponless. Some fled and some were killed—Ugh! by Macer and his men."

He had never seen men fight to kill before, this Tain, and liked it little now that he had seen it. As to the spear-throwing, guards and volunteers alike had been armed with two spears to each man, one for throwing and one for close quarter work, while as many shields

132

as could be made in time had been distributed among these same volunteers.

"How comes it about that you would not wait for me to join you?" I inquired.

"Lord," he answered, "I halted them and waited at a distance from where Macer had his men, and there watched eagerly for your coming to lead us. But Macer's spies told him of our coming, and he advanced against us. Then I had to bid my men fight, for being untrained they could not be trusted to retreat."

This I knew; try to get untrained men to retreat before a superior enemy, and the result is a mere helter-skelter flight.

"And then?" I asked.

"Then I ordered a charge, having warned them to keep each one spear, and to hurl none until they were close on their enemies. I know they would not stand to be charged, so led them, and every man hurled his first spear too soon, and uselessly. Macer's men roared laughter at them, and charged to meet them. Then, being frightened, they threw each his second spear for all that I could say, save for some few that fought bravely at the onset and were killed. The rest fled, some to escape and some to be caught and speared as they ran."

"And you too escaped," I commented. There seemed nothing else to be said over the sorry business—I could imagine the swift result of such a fight, if fight it could be called.

"Lord," said Tain, "I was but one. I stand to be slain by your magic or punished as you may desire."

He was one of those who had seen the shooting in the council hall, and his courage in thus surrendering himself—for he obviously expected death in consequence of the defeat—won my admiration. I laid my hand on his shoulder, and felt him trembling—his will could not quite control his nerves.

"Tain," I said, "if there be any fault, it is my own, for my absence lost our fight. When the tale of the folly of your men is laid before Ner-Ag, your king, there shall be told with it how one man, Tain, played a brave and skilful part. And for you there shall surely be some reward."

He stared as if unable to believe my words, and then

would have dropped on one knee before me, but I stopped him.

"That only to Ner-Ag, the king," I said, "and there is work for us. First catch me one of these, all of you," and I pointed to the stray figures who still drifted past us to eastward.

They rounded up one with little difficulty. Tain disowned him as not coming from among the beaten volunteers, and the man confessed himself deserter.

"Tell all the truth of Macer's men and Macer," I bade, "and I set you free to yield to the king and gain pardon. But if it be not the truth—bid the guards catch me another, Tain—I will blast you dead."

Tain set five of the guards to round up another of the deserters, and when they brought him in his tale confirmed that of the first man. Eina had come from Kir-Asa, bearing some message over which Macer and Neray had quarrelled—Neray had been heard to threaten that he would go back and surrender himself, which had made the men of the king's lands uneasy. Partly to pacify them by loot, and partly to secure their allegiance by making them active participants in his revolt, Macer bade them sack Ag's house, and pay special attention to the wine-casks and vats. Many had got drunk, but they still had great stores of wine.

Then came messengers from the king's lands, telling how we had burnt the palace, Macer tried too late to stop this news from becoming generally known, and his force began to melt—I gathered from what these men told that he had fully a thousand men before the rot set it, this even after allowing from the over-estimate likely to be made by such as our informants. Fully half of these had got themselves too drunk to move when the news of the volunteers' approach was brought in by spies, and at that news Macer fired Ag's house with his own hand—as Watkins and I had fired his, I thought —and got his men together to face the volunteers. He had still about two-thirds of his original force left.

The story of the fight we knew. But these men told us that Macer, himself none too sober, then, and judging his men firmly bound to him by their burning of Ag's house and the slaughter among the volunteers, had in his exuberance over the victory read out Ag's proclamation to his army, jeering at Ag, and promising

134

reward to the man who could suggest the most painful form of death for him, when caught.

It was a false move. There were some among these men who saw that Ag's leniency and offer of unconditional pardon were available only for a few days more, after which they ran the risk of accompanying Macer down the crater of Kir. They expressed their preference for making terms with Ag, rather than adhering to this man, by desertions; it seemed to them, from Macer's reckless excesses, that he was careless whether he won or lost in the end. So it seemed to the two we caught, and so it must have seemed to many more, for, when these two deserted, Macer had hardly a quarter of his men left, and these had gone back to Ag's wine-casks.

Thus the story, identical from both sources, that we learned before we let the deserters go. What had chanced since their desertions, of course, we had yet to learn. There was more of a moon than on the preceding night, and we went on in the moonlight toward the glow that had been Ag's house, keeping ourselves in the shadows as much as possible, to find how the position now stood.

THE RESERVE FORCE

We had gone but a little way in the moonlight when I called a halt and gathered the six who had come with me, together with Tain, round me. Suddenly I had realised that, in place of the army of two hundred men to put against Macer, I had only these. In our plans Watkins and I, relying too much on the volunteers and—as it had proved—too much on the chance of desertions from Macer's force, had omitted to specify when we should unite our forces. He trusted the west to me, while after the burning of the country palace he would hold the king's lands in case Macer should out-march me and my men. We had planned, as the real object of the little campaign, that with the volunteers I should drive Macer and any men who adhered to him on to Watkins with the guards—and now I had nothing left with which to drive.

This I explained fully, and sent back two, the one
135

who had guided us and one other, to tell Watkins that there was no longer a volunteer force, and I had but five men left. As to shooting, with both rifle and revolver I had one hundred and thirty-nine rounds, forty-nine for the revolver and ninety for the rifle; if only two hundred men still stuck to Macer, and I never missed a man, still in the end my power of blasting with thunder would leave him with over fifty followers—against us six.

The two set off at once; Tain and I went on with the other four. We came out to the great road, and from it turned up the avenue to what had been Ag's house. Where Watkins, Bent, and I had been met by the white-clad major-domo, an indistinct heap that looked like fabrics of some sort lay half in the moonlight and half in the shadows cast by the trees. When we came nearer, we saw that it was a pile of bodies, gashed and battered about in sheer devilry, and left as token of the way Macer chose to deal with those who opposed him.

There were men of Ag's establishment, old women, and little children of both sexes—I could guess what had befallen the younger women. There were heads crushed in by repeated blows, children's bodies hacked and disfigured, severed limbs tossed on the pile—there could not have been less than fifty lives represented in that awful heap, and I guessed at once why it was there for us to see. Macer, alarmed at the continual desertions, had determined to bind to himself such men as he had left, by deeds that Ag would never forgive. Probably he had first maddened his followers with drink, and then had urged them on to slaughter, until they needed no more urging, but became as fiendish as was Macer himself. Not even he would instigate so awful a deed as this purposelessly; by it he secured a bodyguard with which, given luck he might yet overawe the country. Its people were in the main unfitted even to defend themselves, owing to centuries of peace; perhaps after a very little experience of this sort of thing they would be only to glad to hand over Ag and his people as the price of cessation. Meanwhile such a terrible measure of action as this would put an end to desertions—so Macer must have seen it, I thought.

The sight of these hacked and dismembered bodies

moved me to black fury. Tain actually wept with rage, and the four guardsmen were almost sick with horror at the sight. We moved on, past the still glowing embers of Ag's burnt-out mansion, and beyond it saw that more burning was being carried on a little over a mile away. Toward this we advanced, guided as much by the yells and laughter which came clearly borne on the still night air as by the flames.

Beyond the trees and shrubs surrounding Ag's house we came to open, cultivated land, and so saw what was afoot. Macer's men were capering like demons in the light thrown by burning huts, and I could guess the fate of the occupants. By the term of his "decree," Macer was not due to begin laying waste to the land until next morning, but already he and his men had far exceeded his original threats.

I had a mind to try the effect of rifle fire on the pillagers, in spite of being so short of ammunition. Thus we six went carefully, feeling fairly safe even in the clear moonlight, since the glare of the burning huts rendered it unlikely that the men would see anything approaching. When we got near, we bent forward on hands and knees so that the young corn hid us; at a distance of about a hundred and fifty yards I signed to my men to halt and lie down flat; it was as near as I dared approach. There is a big difference between such an echoing roar as our revolver shots made in the council hall, and the thin, sharp crack of a rifle fired in the open. These pillaging fiends, half-drunk as they evidently were, might be very little scared, and might even charge toward the shooting—I was by no means sure of them. If they should charge, I wanted to be at such a distance as would enable me to pick off two or three of them, reserving a full magazine, as they came at us. This, I calculated, would scare them from closing, and then rifle magazine and revolver would put them to flight and give me time to reload.

It was an extreme range from which to fire. Even at close quarters, shooting by moonlight is risky work, and at this distance I knew it was most uncertain. I broke open a packet of ammunition and put the loose cartridges in my pocket, took out the magazine to assure myself it was fully charged, snapped the magazine back in place, and loaded the barrel from my pocket. Then, getting the rifle to my shoulder, I found the foresight—a more difficult matter in the moonlight than one might think—and aimed at the nearer of two still figures standing in the light of the flames, with a hope that it might be Macer himself. The shrill, despairing shrieks of women broke out as I pressed the trigger—and saw that I had missed my aim.

My men shrank at the crack of the rifle, but it produced no effect at all on the figures in the firelight. The noise they made may have led them to think, never having heard such a sound before, that it was a distant crash as the ruins of Ag's mansion collapsed yet farther. I jerked the rifle bolt open and back, flinging out the empty shell; I laid another cartridge on the magazine cut-off plate, anxious to get in another shot before the fiends in the firelight detected our presence—and the cartridge jammed in the chamber, the rifle bolt stuck, half-closed.

I tried to pull it open, to close it fully; I tapped it both with my hand and with the revolver butt. The light was too poor for me to risk extreme force on it, but all that I dared do, I did, and still it stuck. More screams of agony came from where the flame of the burning huts was dying down, and I could guess what was going forward there. I had a mind to make a charge with these five men, trusting to the revolver to carry us through.

"Lord," Tain whispered as he lay beside me, "let me go to fight them with my spear, while you send them death by thunder."

The recklessly brave proposal, inspired by the sounds we heard and the piled bodies we had seen, was futile as my own idea of charging—we could not hope to wipe out two hundred devils, heartened by the defeat of the volunteers and rendered careless by the drink with which Macer had plied them. We should but add our own deaths, uselessly, to such as must ensue.

And yet something must be done, or Macer and his fellow demons would pursue their course of slaughter and destruction. Lacking Watkins, and knowing him to be not less than three days' march distant—including the time it would take for my messengers to reach him—I felt helpless. I whispered to my men to retreat; we crawled back until I judged it safe for us to stand,

and then walked on to the shelter of the trees surrounding the ruins of Ag's mansion. I was heartsick at leaving Macer and his men at their bloody work, and felt, too, that these men with me must now lose faith in the power of the stranger, since I could not longer blast offenders to death with thunder. Was I to wait here while Macer spoiled Ag's province, or go back to Watkins, leaving the spoilers at their work?

We came on food from the mansion, which Macer's men had pillaged and abandoned, heaps of it. We ate, out of sight of the pile of dead. By the time we had finished that meal I had come to a decision. We regained the great road in the moonlight—it was early, yet—and I turned to where a cleft in the western skyline marked the entrance to the valley by which Watkins, Bent and I had come to Kir-Asa, the defile leading to the place where ghosts chase women.

We marched on, and as we went I told Tain my plan for I needed his authority, as an officer of the guard, to back my own. After a couple of hours of steady tramping we came to the escarpment beyond the canal, and a little further on a woman stepped forward from the rock-shelter where we three had found food at the exit from the defile. She stood still with hand upraised to warn us against advancing further, and a couple of great apes ambled clumsily round her, at times resting on their forepaws to look up at her face as if they waited her commands. She was very much like her predecessor, with a similar angry expression—it showed even in the moonlight, and gave me an odd sense of recognition of her, though I had never seen her before. This gift of controlling the apes ran only in the women of one group of families.

"Stay," she bade threateningly. "Without the graven sign of the king you may not pass here."

"We would not pass," I said, "but seek to speak with you."

"Then stand, and say on," she bade, bending to caress one of her uncouth attendants.

"Tain, officer of the king's guard, will tell you what has chanced in the land," I said. "Then I will speak with you."

"Nantia," said Tain, "King Saya-Comin is dead, two of his sons are dead, and the third, being mad, lays

139

waste the lands of this western border, killing its men and giving its women to his men, because Ner-Ag sits king in Kir-Asa."

"Is this truth?" the Nantia asked wonderingly—she was of a race that never so much as dreamed of war.

"The madmen have burned the house of Ner-Ag in the lands below," Tain said, "and before the ruins lie a heap of slain, men and children and old women of Ner-Ag's people." He went into details over the contents of that heap, and over the fate of the younger women.

"Then what would you—what seek you of me?" the Nantia asked when all the tale was told.

I took a step forward. "I, Jack, husband to Eve of the house of Ner-Ag, king, would command your aid," I said.

"Mine?" she asked incredulously. Then she took note of the title I had claimed, and since I was backed by an escort of the royal guards, she bowed before me.

"Yours, Nantia," I said. "You shall gather together your beasts and lead them down into Ner-Ag's lands, there to loose them that they may tear in pieces those who violate women and slay children. This I lay on you as the decree of Ner-Ag, your king."

She bowed again, never thinking of questioning the royal authority, by which she held her place. "Now, or at dawn?" she asked.

"Now," I told her, "for even at this hour women are suffering and men being slain."

She turned toward the hills and sent forth a cry that went echoing up the defile. "Lords," she bade us, "come you close about me, lest my guardians of the way take you for my foes."

I, for one, was glad enough to comply with the request. The Nantia cried to the hills again, then looked closely at each of us in turn, stroked our faces and arms, and made little caressing noises, while her two constant attendants stalked round us, sometimes almost upright and sometimes on all fours, watching the performance closely. With time to observe the beasts at leisure, I saw that they were ordinary apes, probably orang-outang, but very large even for that breed.

Presently there came an uncanny rustling and

movement all about us, and I felt afraid as the great beasts, in response to their mistress' call, swarmed round, indistinct in the moonlight against the brown rock background. I wondered what would happen if by chance the Nantia should lose control over them, and that still more when she asked:

"Lord, must it be? Even now they thieve from the fields until the people murmur against me, and if I myself lead them across the fields, then will they thieve still more."

"Yet must it be," I said, "or all the province will be laid waste, and there will be left neither crops nor people to murmur against theft."

"Then let us go," she said.

And, as we made to move, she called to her pack as a man might call his dogs. The monkeys lumbered on with us, chattering among themselves, getting in our way, running on ahead and turning back to see if their mistress were coming. Their half-human faces looked fierce and ugly in the moonlight, and I thought of Watkins' theory of evolution, and the "things of the waste" we had seen beyond the defile.

"Do you not fear—the valley beyond the pass?" I asked the woman.

She smiled. "With such a guard I fear nothing," she said. "Night and day they attend me—they wakened me at your coming—and except that a man might slay my guard and me by magic, as might chance anywhere in the land and did chance to the Nantia who was before me, I am safe as in the royal palace at Kir-Asa."

I wondered how she could accept such a fate as this solitary existence. Possibly the gift of control over the beasts bred liking for her uncanny task.

I led her down by way of the great road to where all that was left of Ag's house still smouldered. By the heap of dead, at sight of which the Nantia cried aloud, the chattering of her monkeys grew to jabbering and angry growling as the smell of blood excited them. They wanted to stay, to sniff and paw the dead bodies, and with that intent they crowded and pushed at each other round the grisly pile, so that their mistress had difficulty in persuading them from it. This she did with shrill, angry cries, and with kicks—strange it was to see the great brutes, any one of which could have torn her

141

in pieces in an instant, cower away and whimper at her scolding.

Beyond the shrubs surrounding the house, in the open ground across which I had advanced when the rifle jammed, we came within a hundred yards of a figure that turned away from us and ran yelling toward where we had seen the reed huts burning. I guessed this to be a sentry posted by Macer, or he may have been a man from among the rebels returning to Ag's house on the chance of more loot, or a last deserter before day should put desertion out of the question by leading to fresh excesses. Regarding this, there could be no certainty, either then or after.

A confusion of cries ensued as Macer's men, who had been sleeping on the scene of their last orgy, wakened each other at the alarm. The moon was near on its setting now. It hung over the hills of the western border, lighting the figures of Macer's men and the terrible army of the Nantia, beside whom we six walked closely. I felt little thrills of horror, but no pity—we had too lately passed by the heap of dead for that. I knew, too, that there would be captured women among Macer's men, but it was impossible to save them—perhaps kinder not to save them, considering how they would be viewed after this night's work, by the standpoint of their race. In any case there was no possibility of parley, I felt—Macer had put himself and his fellows beyond that. So I gave the word:

"Loose them to slay, Nantia, and to slay on while one remains alive."

She bowed her acquiescence. Her apes were already restless from the smell of blood and sight of the bodies in Ag's garden, and now she urged them on, pointing to where Macer's men huddled, too frightened either to defend themselves or flee. Her cries struck on my ears as almost familiar—they were exactly such cries as those with which her predecessor had set the beasts on us three, when we came out from the defile toward Kir-Asa.

Of what followed, I have no intention of telling. I sat upon the ground with my hands over my ears, trying to shut out the sounds of that—I would have said battle, but it was mere ruthless extermination. Then I remembered that before these people I must at any cost preserve the dignity my station demanded, and forced myself to stand and watch. Thus do I know by actual sight how the fiends in hell find diversion, and of what nature is the torment of damned souls.

"Call them off, Nantia," I said at last, for she stood silent in sheer horror, and I could see that her beasts had begun to quarrel over the worrying and tossing of dead bodies.

At that she roused herself and called the apes back to her. I feared, at first, lest they should fall on us, but they came fawning round their mistress at her cry, and she spoke commendingly to them, patting and stroking their bloody heads. They settled to comparative quiet, being content and sated with their work.

"If we six stay here while you return, is it safe for us?" I asked her.

"Fully safe," she answered. "They have seen you with me, and any that come near you will smell my touch on you. They are wiser than the lower brutes."

I thought, after what we had seen, that except for men turned evil there could be no lower brutes than these.

"Take them back, then," I bade. "And as for you, Nantia, it is for Ner-Ag, king, to reward you for your aid, when the tale of how your beasts saved the people of this province is laid before him."

"If I might ask," she said timidly, "I would have that more food be sent, that my beasts may not so much seek to thieve from the fields of the plain."

"This, too, shall be done," I promised. "Take them, and go."

They lumbered past us as she bade them follow her, jabbering, mouthing, sniffing, like the shapes of an evil dream.

EINA

If I felt inclined to question my own right to order that awful vengeance on Macer's men, I had but to consider the possible alternatives. At the least, three days must elapse before Watkins could bring up the guards, and in that time Macer might have destroyed

143

nearly half this western province, possibly gaining strength as they went on—and I had five men and a jammed rifle with which to oppose them. And—for Macer's final overthrow was inevitable in any case—he and his men were doomed ultimately to go living into the fiery crater of Kir; I had prevented that, though, by a death not less terrible. So far as I could see, the aid on which I had seized was most economical of life and suffering, in the long run, and therefore mine had been the best course to adopt.

We six slept where the Nantia and her monkeys left us. The moon was dropping behind the western hills when the last of the beasts straggled past, hastening after their companions. I lay for awhile, staring up at the sky in utter exhaustion. Then I must have rolled over on my side and slept, for the sun-rays wakened me, wet with dew and chilled by the drop in temperature that comes with dawn. I sat up to see my five companions still stretched out like dead men around me, for they too had been utterly tired out.

The sun shining on Tain's face wakened him, and he sat up, shivering. "Lord," he asked, "what shall we do now—return?"

"Not yet," I answered. "First, even before we eat, now that we have light to see we must go there"—I pointed to the scene of last night's horrors—"that we may take back sure tidings of Macer's end."

At that he roused the guardsmen, and we went to our grisly task. The guards turned over for me every body that did not lie so as to admit of full inspection, and there were more than three hundred, including those of the captured women. Of the state in which we found them, the less said the better; I had to look closely at every one of them, and, in spite of disfigurements, I was certain at the end of the search that neither Macer, Neray nor Eina was among them.

Here was an ugly set-back. Had Macer more men with him than I had thought—was there another party of raiders, more dangerous than this by reason of the presence of its directing brain, still to be dealt with? However this might be, I knew our work was not yet ended, and thus, on the way back to the ruins of Ag's house to look for food, I stopped out in the open—so that we might have timely warning of any attack on us—and got the jammed cartridge out of my rifle. It was little trouble by daylight; a few taps with the revolver butt got the bolt open, and the cartridge dropped out. I concluded my task by examining the rest of the cartridges carefully, and discarding one other that looked a trifle unsafe.

With a sound rifle again, I felt more at ease. We went back to Ag's place, and there was food scattered about in plenty, though we had to drive the flies off it. In spite of what the last few hours had shown us, we were not squeamish over a few flies, and ate our fill, still reserving the dried meat rations we carried in case of emergency.

After the meal, while I sat cogitating—well to windward of the pile of dead—Tain came to me.

"Lord," he said, "I have found one—will you come and see?"

I went with him beyond a little thicket of shrubs, and there, almost hidden in the greenery, lay the corpse of Neray. All round him the turf was trampled and the branches of shrubs broken down, as if there had been a savage struggle, and on his throat were finger-marks. Macer, I guessed, had choked the life out of him to prevent his going back to surrender himself to Ag. But was this after or before we set the apes on his men? Had Macer and Neray been hidden here when we passed, and where now was Eina?

Bending down, I put a hand on Neray's breast, under his tunic—my men recoiled at the act, as if it were a fearful thing for me to do, though they themselves had turned over the corpses of Macer's men for my inspection, without hesitation. I did not know how long it takes for a corpse to grow cold, but I could feel that this body still retained some warmth.

From this I knew that no other force of raiders remained for us to deal with. Macer and Neray—and perhaps Eina with them—had either been separated from the main body when the Nantia bade her beasts attack, or else the three of them had fled in time. Here they had concealed themselves; here Macer and Neray had quarrelled—perhaps Neray had attempted to go to the blue-uniformed guards he saw with me in order to surrender himself—and Macer had strangled him in a fierce fight. I felt a sense of gratitude over our own

145

escape. Had he dared, Macer might have slaughtered the six of us while we slept in the open, exhausted and unguarded as we were.

And now, I judged, Macer alone was left. I recalled the ultimate threat of his proclamation; his deeds so far had shown that this was no mere threat without intent to act, and Neray, lying dead here, indicated where I must look for Macer. But first, I must report to Watkins. I sent three of the guards, since none of them seemed quite certain of the way back, and judged that where the memory of one might be at fault another would retain enough impression of the route to guide his fellows.

"Go back to the main body of the guard," I bade, "claim audience with their chief, having in your journey kept to the way by which we came. When you have audience with Philip, kinsman to Ner-Ag, tell him that no man follows Macer now, for all are destroyed. Then tell him that I follow on Macer's heels, since he alone is left alive, and that while he lives I will not cease from following."

I made each man repeat the message in the hearing of his fellows, and sent them off. Watkins could use his own discretion—I knew enough of him to foretell that he would cross-question each one of these fellows until he had every detail of what we had seen and done, and thus the bare message was enough. Meanwhile both Watkins and the guards were three days distance from me. They could come and join in the round-up—supposing that it was not all over by the time they arrived—if Watkins chose. This I left to him, and meanwhile, having regard to Macer's threat regarding the "things of the waste," I could not remain inactive. It would be the height of folly to sit down and wait till Watkins and the guards should come, or to hope that the ghosts—or whatever they might be—were harmless, and Macer thus incapable of working further evil in the land.

Now, the three men being gone, I turned again toward the pass in the hills. From Ag's look of fear when he read out the proclamation Macer had sent to him, and from the dread which made these "things of the waste" a forbidden subject among the women of the country, I had not the slightest doubt that Macer would head straight for the place where ghosts chase women, thence—as he and all his people believed possible—to lead the dread beings to the destruction of the country's women. If I had questioned whether he would not even now stay his hand and turn back to surrender, there was the still warm corpse of Neray as answer to the question, with the deeply indented finger-marks on its throat.

With Tain and the one guardsman remaining as our attendant, I came to the Nantia shelter some time before noon, and there stopped to eat with her. She had store of food enough for days to come, and thus in spite of the devastation of the country nearest to her I had no compunction in taking from her stock. While we ate, I explained our errand, and saw just such a look of fear as I remembered on Ag's face, when I spoke of Macer's threat and the probability of his having gone through to the valley beyond the defile in her absence.

She agreed that there was a probability of this having happened. "Because of my children"—for so she called them—"I returned slowly—I had to call them continually from thieving in the corn. The sun was high when we reached this place again."

The maize was just showing its tassels in the corn lands, and I could guess how the apes would break away to steal the green kernels and suck out the sweet sap from the growing grain. Outside the rock shelter the Nantia's two especial pets lazed in the warmth; one of them licked a spear wound, token of the part he had played in the night's adventure. They were indifferent to us whom the Nantia had stroked and caressed as friends.

It was my intention, after eating, to go on to the valley and trust to my rifle to end the work the monkeys had carried so far. I sat with Tain, eating, and the Nantia watched us.

"I have in mind to ask Ner-Ag, the king, to build you a sound dwelling of stone," I told her. "So shall you have a place to store your food apart, a place to sleep, and a place whence you may look out to guard the way of the pass. It would be better than this rough shelter."

Her eyes sparkled with pleased anticipation. "But

147

why this for me, Lord?" she asked.

"Because, when I spoke of rewarding you for your aid, you asked only food for the beasts," I answered. "It is fitting that you too receive according to the measure of your service."

In place of answering she stood and looked along the way we had come. Following her gaze, I saw one approaching swiftly, and when that one came nearer I recognized Eina, the woman who had brought Macer's proclamation to Kir-Asa. I stepped out to bar her from advancing—her presence was proof that I had guessed rightly: Macer had gone through the defile to the valley beyond.

"What seek you here, Eina?" I asked her.

She looked steadily at me, recognising me as having been in the council hall when she brought her message to Ner-Ag. I had seen her as weary then, but now she looked ill with fatigue, and to the utter despair that had engraved itself on her face since she made herself outcast for Macer's sake was added the last evil—fear.

"Him whom I serve," she answered, stonily calm. "I would save him from the sin that shall not be forgiven, and would die with him."

The unselfish love of a woman has many forms of expression, and here was one that claimed respect. The man, utterly forgetful of her welfare, went in intent to a sin past forgiveness in this world and that to come; the woman followed to serve and die with him, thinking of him only.

"It is too late," I told her as gently as possible. "He is already in the valley."

"There, until night comes, he must wait," she said, "and in the hours of day I may win him from his purpose, that he may die with no more against him than is now. The things of the waste will not come to him by day until they have communed with him by night and grown hungry to follow his leading."

"What would you do?" I asked, wondering at her.

She gazed steadily at me, and her lip trembled until she answered. "For this man's sake," she said, "I put aside speech with my people, forsook my child, braved the doom that is my merit, to live when death would be a gift past price. This through my love for him, and where we love we seek to serve, and to guard from all

148

evil. Evil through his madness has he wrought, and by
reason of his working evil has come on him. Yet even
now he is guiltless in deed of this his most evil intent. I
would have you let me pass to him, that by my love I
may prevail on him to turn away from the things of
the waste. To prevail over him lest he do this last
horror, I will lie to him, telling him that now all is past
he may surrender himself and hope for pardon from
Ner-Ag, or that with me he may flee beyond this land
to safety. Thus, I will plead with him, not that he may
in truth win pardon or escape, but that, being doomed,
he may die as the king's son, and not as worse than
beast seeking the destruction of my sisters who have
not sinned—as for him I have sinned."

"And when you have turned him from his purpose,
what then?" I asked. Her strength of purpose and utter
sincerity moved me deeply, but I could not see the
practical outcome of this.

"If I go on to the valley, and find him there," she
answered, "then will I speak with him and win him to
my way. When I have turned him to my will, then will
I raise my hand, thus"—and she raised her right hand
to full stretch above her head—"and then, if you
advance to take him, and he kill me, so shall I escape
the punishment of life laid on me by the decree of
Ner-Ag. Or if it is your will that I should endure, then
can you blast him with thunder so that he die suddenly
as his brothers died, and there shall be an end of these
things."

I considered it. If she found Macer and brought him
into my view, the rifle would do the rest at anything
short of half a mile. I could go with her to the entrance
to the valley, and if she were sincere in her desire to
win Macer to repentance, an hour or less would be
enough. I had not one second's doubt of her sincerity;
one look at her face was enough to tell her earnestness,
and one thought of the nature of Macer's threat
enough to convince regarding any woman's desire to
turn him from his course.

"I will come with you to the valley entrance, and
there wait your signal," I told her.

She bowed before me. "Lord," she said, for the first
time using the title, "if it were given to me to speak
with my people again, I would bid them do reverence

149

to you for your mercy to my man and to me."

"If I can compass it, Eina," I said, "when all this is past I will try to find you a place from which you may speak with all, and find life not so much a burden to be feared." For I had a thought that with Eve's gentle sympathy and aid this might be done.

But Eina shook her head. "I have sown—I reap," she said. "Now let me take food and drink to bear to the valley, and go while the sun is still high."

The Nantia, who had heard all, brought out food and a small jar of water, and set them down, retiring again within her shelter—she would not approach nor speak with Eina. Eina took up the food, and with the three of us following set out on her way after a sip at the contents of the jar. I felt half inclined to bid her rest and eat here, but there was the Nantia's attitude toward her, and there was, too, such eagerness on her part to set about her task that I felt certain she would have refused the delay.

We went with her up into the defile, and in passing the rock where the other Nantia had died I saw that all traces of the beasts we had shot had been cleared away. Toward the entrance to the valley we fell back, letting Eina go on alone. She was past all earthly sense of fear, for no other woman of the country would have dared advance beyond the Nantia's shelter toward this valley. She went on as if the things of the waste had no existence. While we moved forward cautiously, taking cover behind successive rocks to keep ourselves hidden from anyone in the valley before us, she disappeared beyond the end of the pass. We crawled up carefully, keeping to the rock-strewn ground beside the trace of the great road, and came to the last light rise beyond which the natural amphitheatre of the valley showed clearly.

Down by one of the flat rocks, barely three hundred yards distant, were Macer and Eina seated, and I could see that he was eating the food she had brought. Twice I saw him push her away roughly, and guessed that he was resisting her advances. He finished eating; the sound of her voice came to us as a faint murmur, and I saw her place her hand on his arm. Then like a wild beast he flung himself upon her, so that they rolled struggling on the ground. I had my rifle loaded and ready, and raised my head with a shout at which he flung the woman aside and stood up, looking round, while Eina lay quite still. I fired, and saw the bullet splash on the rock behind, nearly a yard wide of its mark.

He ran toward the hillside, and I missed again. With a fervent wish that Watkins, sure shot that he was, had been here, I took a long breath and waited with my finger on the trigger while Macer set about the ascent of the steep slope, which, steadying his pace, made him a surer target. Then again I either altogether missed him, or wounded him so slightly as not to arrest his progress, and with the next shot I brought him down. He flung up his arms, came over backward toward us, and rolled some way down the hillside. There his body hung limply, curved over a rock out-crop, with arms dangling lifelessly.

We ran to where Eina lay, and I knelt beside her, blaming myself for having let her go, while Tain stood and looked at her with tears streaming down his face. I could see that she was quite dead. The fiend she had tried to save from his last devilry had broken her neck with his savage grip.

Death had been kind to her, though. All the lines that her doom of continuing life had set on her face were gone, and gone, too, was the soiling mark of her sin. Her eyes, not wide and staring as is common in dead faces, but half-closed, seemed to tell that she rested at last, and her lips just parted in a smile of content. Had she seen this as her way of escape, when she begged me to let her take it?

"Tain," I said, "let us bear her hence. It is not fitting that she should be left here."

He bowed his assent. "I myself will carry her, lord," he answered, "but what of that?" and he pointed to where Macer's body hung among the rocks of the hillside.

"There let it hang for the kites to peck, till the bones drop down to the valley." I answered.

Then, Tain carrying the body of Eina in his arms—she was thin and wasted, and no great weight—we went back, in the knowledge that Macer's revolt was at an end.

Before we went down to the plain, at the edge of

the escarpment from which one may first view Kir-Asa
on coming to this land, we dug a deep grave with the
help of the Nantia and such tools as she had, and
placed Eina's body in it, for once ignoring the custom
of the country in burning its dead. There she lies,
overlooking the land whose women she would have
saved from the man for whose worthless love she
wrecked her life.

CONCERNING IOHN WATKYNS AND COMPANIONS

Some way along the great road, where we were able
to find people who could spread the news of the end
of Macer and his raiders and so prevent flight from the
western province, we made a halt for the night.
Already many had fled, but our news stopped the rest,
and I had no doubt that, in a few days, the inhabitants
would have settled again. In the morning, Tain found
one of the rickshaw-like conveyances of the country,
like those in which Ag had first taken us to Kir-Asa. He
unearthed this, produced two men to pull it, and was
waiting for me at dawn with not a little pride in his
achievement.

"Where are the others?" I asked him.

"The others, lord?" he questioned, puzzled. "Two
men can pull all the way."

"No, Tain, the other wheeled chairs," I said. "We
three—you, this man of the guard, and I, shared such
small perils as were while Macer lived. We three will go
in equal fashion to Kir-Asa, whether it be on wheels or
on our feet."

After that, I might have bidden Tain and our
follower of the guard hang themselves, or anything else
I liked—there was nothing in their power that they
would not have done for me. Tain found two more
rickshaws, and the rest of the journey was both easy
and dignified.

It was not a great distance beyond Ag's mansion
that we took to wheels, for the first day was far spent
when we had buried Eina and bidden the Nantia
good-bye. Anxious as I was to get back to Eve, I was
both physically and mentally exhausted. For weeks,
now, I had been subjected to alternations of every sort

of emotion, all on high notes, and now I desired nothing but to get back to my princess and with her to rest, leaving Watkins to plan our time and way of leaving the country, if he chose. For myself I could plan no more, as yet—I refused even to think of the future and all that lay between us and a safe return to the lands of our own people.

In that sort of mood, at sunset, I bade our men turn off from the road, realising that it was useless to hope to reach Kir-Asa that night. I directed them toward a building of grey stone to the right of the road, and an old man standing by the entrance to the building watched us descend from our conveyances.

"We seek food and rest for the night," I said to him. "If you need explanation of why we travel, this officer of the guard will give it—after we have rested awhile."

It was not a very gracious way of requesting a night's lodging, but the old man bade us come within quite courteously, neither asking our names nor offering to tell his own—he seemed quite incurious about us. I noted that Tain looked a little uncomfortable, and, when our host had left the room to which he conducted us, questioned the cause.

"This man was Eina's father," he answered. "I would have told you, had I known your intent to come here."

"It was not intent, but mere chance," I said, "for this place looked easy of access and fit to shelter us well. We must tell him of her end, though."

Then this Tain won my warmest approval. Knowing that I was very tired, he went himself to the old man and told the story of Eina's death and of her attempt to save Macer from the last evil he wrought. Presently the old man came to me.

"Lord, rest in my house in peace," he said, "and let me count it some little return for that which, in service to my daughter, you have done for me." And he went out to mourn over her end as he had been forced to grieve over her life, so that we did not see him again. There were two serving-men, as old as their master, who attended to our needs.

Retiring early to the room allotted, I wakened early. The dim light of the single lamp had provided little chance of observing the room closely. But, in the morning, I saw that the wall of the room facing the curtained aperture—and that unusually small—which served as window, was curiously decorated. A second glance showed me that the decoration was English script, cut in the stone as had been the writing in the cave, and by the same hand. Here, however, "Iohn Watkyns" had had more time. Whether he had cut this record as direction to any who might follow, or whether he had done it merely to pass a weary time, I do not know. Probably the latter, though.

The script was small. There was much detailed description of the habits of the people—which had not changed, apparently, between that time and now—and also much concerning the fauna of the country, including a "curious ratt" which we had not observed. Also John had noted that "they have many mungeese" (a word which at the last I identified with "mongoose," an animal with which service in the East India Company would have made John familiar) "by which the land is kept purged of serpents." There was a remark on the wonders of Kir-Asa, but no mention of its stores of metal. I concluded that the old adventurer had not seen the gold in the store-house, or he would hardly have let that pass without remark. On the other hand he mentioned that "these people have much emerylds, which they string for necklaces, but oft break in the boring. They are great stones of much value." Eve's necklace, which she regarded as of little account, suddenly went up in my estimation.

He spoke the language, this dead pioneer, "which for a Watkyns is easy of learning, since it is much like the heathen dialects which through service with the Company (the East India Company) I acquired, as do most of the men of my name and family." Then came a line that spoke of despair: "Because of the drunkenness of Van den Heuvel, and his violence when he is in liquor, through which he did offer insult to one of these heathen women, have I been imprisoned here these three months, and we all kept separate. Must I endure to look on these walls till death do bring release."

Beneath this a wavering mark was scratched on the stone, as if the author would indicate a break in the time of his inscribing. After that, in fainter, lighter marking, came the story of "Iohn Watkyns, gent.," as he subscribed his name to this strange diary.

"It is more than a yeer that I last wrote upon this wall, and how many mighty marvels have been since that time. There was the erupting of this volcano, and the death of the man they called king, after his madness when he broak from restraint and ran about the city, none daring to lay hands on him since he was the king, and yet they made a great to-do when he broak his neck and so died. Likewise I was wedded after their fashion (for being heathen and knowing nothing of the true Godd they do not marry as do Xtian people, but most hastily and without proper ceremonies, yet are their women most vertuous) to a most tender and beautiful lady, for whose sake I had no mind to leave this land, but to stay with its people and see if by any fashion I might improve them, sending messengers to my brother Philip. But now is my wife dedd of bearing me a child, the which I have left with her father to care for, and so go, not caring greatly if the gulph and the trembling bridge do make an end of me. And most strange it is to be in this place where I was kept prisoner for near on the half of a yeer, and to feel that with my companions (all save Peter Sluys, who was bit by a serpent) I may go hence in peace and honour."

My ordinary note-book had long since gone to pulp in the spray of the trembling bridge, but I still had a flat waterproof wallet, with about a score of sheets of thin notepaper. One of these had on it the message inscribed in the cave, and another the decree of Kirtas-Asen as Eve had read it out for me, and now on a third I put the story of John Watkins for my Watkins to see. As for me, I thought of Eve waiting at Kir-Asa, and had it not been too early to turn out our drivers, I would not have stayed to take down so much.

But the last sentence of the writings made me curious. If all this were true, if "Iohn Watkyns" and his companions had won "peace and honour" in the country, and left it freely as this writing implied how did it come about that they had to fight with the monkey guard in the pass, where two of them were killed? It occurred to me to ask Tain as we ate if any of the story of these men had been handed down in the country, and if he knew of the writing on the wall.

"Of these scratches on the stone I did not know," he told me, "nor would any man have said that such marks could tell a story, for they are not like our writing, lord. But of the men who came out of the west generations since, as you came, there is a story which my father had from his father, and so from their day."

"Tell me that story, Tain," I bade.

"Their leader married a lady of the house of Ner-Ag, who before had been married with a man of our race, but he died leaving her without children. Then in turn she died, having borne a child to the stranger from the west, and he and his men set out to leave the country.

"Here in this house for a time he lay sick, and the man who then lived here, by whom these men from the west had been guarded as prisoners when they first came, gave place to him and his companions until he should be ready to go on his way. Then one of the men, who was not sick, looked with eyes of unlawful love on the woman of this house, wife to him who gave them all a place here, and she being weak and a woman, yielded herself to him. Then her husband drove her forth, and after these men had gone was a daughter born to her through that man with whom she sinned. Of the stock of that daughter was the old man with whom we spoke last night and Eina, whom we buried on the hill. And, when this sin was known, the men from the west were bidden give up for punishment that one who had thus sinned against the man who sheltered him, but they would not, and so fled. It is known that the one who sinned and one other were torn in pieces by the guard kept by the Nantia on that day, and the others fled to the desert lands beyond."

The brief, tragic story, thus simply told, accounted for Eina's brown hair, and perhaps accounted, too, for her lapse from honour for Macer's sake. As her ancestress had sinned, so had she sinned. Most of the history of "Iohn Watkyns" and his friends was clear, now. Prisoners at first, they had in some way won freedom and some place of worth, while "Iohn" himself had won happiness, for a time. Even when that was ended, they might all have gone forth in safety, but for the evil that one of them brought on his host, violating two of the world's most sacred laws in committing the one crime.

I could account in my own mind now, not so much for Eina's beauty, for this was a country of beautiful women (and in that I saw a provision of nature, since it was a failing race and every device that would increase the stock was to be reckoned in) but for the cast of her features. Thinking back, now, I could see in Eina's way of accepting her fate—the stony calm of it—an exaggeration of the placidity with which a well-bred Hollander will face the trials of life. There are those who say that heredity counts for little in comparison with training, but, with this example of the force of heredity in mind, I disagree. And her whole career was instance of something bred in the bone showing in the flesh. I may exaggerate the coincidences of her life and that of the woman of a century and a half ago, but I saw her, talked with her, and thus I see her, who rests on the brow of the western hill that looks toward Kir-Asa.

We left the house without seeing our host again, and before noon our rickshaw men had pulled us up the incline and through the great gateway of Kir-Asa. I looked up at the mansion in which Eve and I had spent our three days. It was closed now, and vacant pending my return. Then on to the palace, and with Tain and our one attendant man of the guards—whose name, I had been somewhat amused to learn, was Bar-Ug—through the council hall until we three stood before Ner-Ag, king. In accordance with his decree, he sat to administer justice in the second quarter of the day before noon. He did not so much as move a muscle of his face as we three, unshaven and with the dirt that the chase after Macer had left us still on our clothes—ranged before him. He had had no word of our coming.

"O king," I said, "Macer and the men who were with him are dead. When such men as came to supplement the guards had played the fool and fled, I called on the Nantia to aid us with her apes. She led them at my bidding, and now there is nothing left to trouble the peace of the land."

Ag considered it before he replied. He saw us as

157

three tired men, and, knowing the main fact, did not ask for full details then.

"It is well, Jack, son of Faulk," he replied gravely. "Now may you and those with you go to your own places. Over this matter, now it is ended, there shall be no punishments, but I may decree certain rewards when Philip my kinsman has come to me. Of that in its time and in its place."

Thus spoke Ner-Ag, and as he spoke I saw him every inch a king. Not the limited, ineffectual representative of monarchy as that is in the present, but a being of a more generous age and time, a more complete and wise ruler, and a more just interpretation of the word which signifies him who knows, and who knowing is able to safeguard the interests of his people. Ag, as he sat there, was a great man and just; the country had no reason to regret the dissolution of the council of five and the passing of the old order.

I took little time, though, to consider him then. I passed on at his bidding, not staying to note what became of Tain or of Bar-Ug. In one of the state apartments I came on Niala, who put a finger on her lip to enjoin my silence and motioned me to a certain doorway, smiling her welcome at me as she pointed. Again I passed on, this time to the journey's ultimate end.

For there, where Niala had motioned me to enter, was waiting my princess with the shining eyes. Niala told me, after, that for all the time of my absence Eve had waited abstractedly, as if the half of her had been taken away. I know that as her arms closed round me I counted all other things trivial, and of little account——I had lived, since I left her, only for the minute when I might forget the world in the ecstasy of this return.

REWARDS

We went, next day, to the mansion that had been Ag's home, and that he had set apart for our use. First, though, Ag had all the story of Macer's overthrow and his end, hearing the details as much from Eve as from me, so far as I had told her the story. He talked it all out with me the first evening after my return, a family party, and wished Watkins could have been with us. Ag spoke no word of his opinion on the matter; he showed no sign of approval for the way in which Watkins and I had carried the business through, but merely questioned, until he knew what we had seen and done since we marched out from Kir-Asa.

And next day, Eve and I went back to the world apart that was our right, the separateness from outside interests that had made our three days so wonderful—only to find that it was not to endure even for three hours, now. For Watkins, having brought back the guards, looked in on us late in the afternoon, stayed to eat with us, and then stayed on. Neither Eve nor I regretted his presence, though I think we would have resented any other intrusion on us just then. It was Eve, in fact, who told Watkins that he must not go back to the palace till the morning, and bade a messenger go to Ag and say that our guest would sleep here at the mansion. There was something tonic about Watkins, something that braced and cheered us both, although the language of the country—we talked in it since Eve was with us—gave little or no opportunity for his comments on men and things which in English were as illuminating as they were—usually—cynical.

It was growing late when Eve slipped away and left Watkins and me together. I had not mentioned the story of old "Iohn" in her presence, since it was in a way linked up with Tain's story of Eina and her people, and Eve guessed that I wished to tell this part of the story. So she bent to kiss me as might a wife of years' standing, and left us together, from the doorway giving back a smile that bade me not stay too long. Watkins looked after her thoughtfully, and sat down again when she had gone.

"You've won, Faulkner," he said. "I congratulate you without reserve now."

"For the first time?" I asked.

He nodded. "I wasn't sure, before," he answered, "but now I know she'll hold through with you and fit everywhere. You're a very lucky man—be good to her."

"Hardly a necessary caution, as yet," I told him. "But I've found something that will interest you."

The story of old "Iohn" more than interested him; he roared with laughter over his ancestor's idea of improving the race.

"The smug old hypocrite!" he exclaimed. "Just as in these days any European industrialist who found the country would introduce the tape machine and motors, and cash and cheap newspapers. Faulkner, there's nothing left on earth like this little country, and to try and improve it, that way, would be to spoil it."

"It might be improved some ways," I argued.

"Leave it alone," he said, with the satiric set of his face that I knew betokened seriousness. "It's a simple people living in plenty and happiness, without the unrest that follows on civilisation—none of the cash and discount system, none of the frauds and lying that make up what we call business, and where in the world will you find men as clean-thinking, or women as pure? Civilisation could give these people nothing comparable with what it would take away."

"Perhaps not," I said doubtfully. "I was thinking more of what civilisation could gain and learn from the country. The tremendous magnificence of Kir-Asa, the uselessness of gold—there's enough in that store to bring it down to a quarter of what its value is now——"

"Leave Thomas Cook's patrons to gape at the Pyramids and drop their cigarette ends over Niagara," he interrupted.

"Faulkner, can't you hear a crowd of gaping tourists saying, 'Gee, some ape!' at sight of that wonderful monkey guard, and a trade unionist shrieking, 'Long live the freedom of the proletariat!' from in front of Kirtas-Asen's monolith? As for the gold, can't you imagine the little syndicate of international financiers controlling it, doling it out so as to keep up the price and fatten themselves—and the double headline in the morning rag at the suburban breakfast-table, screaming, 'WORLD'S LAST SECRET UNVEILED. CREATION NO LONGER A MYSTERY. BY OUR SPECIAL REPRESENTATIVE'?"

"That's the worse side," I argued weakly.

"Worse?" he echoed. "There'd be worse than that, Faulkner. Here's a contented people under a good king, safe for years from the fret of a world gone mad

160

with mechanical devices for crowding lives and spoiling nerves. While they are safe, for heaven's sake keep out civilisation and the wreckage it would make. Let this little Eden remain without its snake, no matter what that snake might bring or else the next generation of these women will be turning the place where ghosts chase women into a golf course, and yelling 'Fore!' at the Nantia."

"Maybe," I said. That last argument won me.

"Not maybe, but certainly," he urged earnestly. "Faulkner, we may forget it if I don't say it now, or some chance word may slip, if we don't make a firm resolve—let's promise each other that no word from either of us two shall ever give this place over to the financier and the tourist, and drag its people down from their simplicity to the insane complex we call civilisation. I feel strongly on it, and so will you, when you've thought it over."

"I promise, without thinking any more," I agreed.

"And I promise," he said. "Now run off to your Eve, and we'll talk to-morrow."

I needed no second bidding, although the story of Eina that Tain had told me was not yet passed on to him. I left him and went to where Eve waited my coming.

Now Ner-Ag, king, sat on the throne of carven stone before the council table, and the great hall was full, for all who could come had been bidden attend. The three lords of the provinces had been called in, and though this was but the day following that on which Watkins marched in the throng in the council hall was representative of the whole country. Before that assembly, since this was Ag's justice hour, a man of the people stood at the lower end of the council table.

"Ner-Ag, king," he said loudly, "I had a calf that strayed on my neighbour's land, and my neighbour's wife kept the calf. I come before you to ask that it may be restored to me."

"Where is the neighbour?" Ag asked.

"He fled with Macer, and is dead," the man answered.

"And the wife?" Ag asked again.

"Tending her crops, that her husband sowed," said

161

the applicant.

"Has she knowledge of your coming before me to claim the calf?" Ag pursued.

"I myself told her," said the man, a little disturbed by such detailed questioning, "and she told me that I might claim——" He checked himself on the word, as if he feared to say too much.

I saw Ag smile. "A calf is a hungry beast, in green corn," he observed.

A little ripple of laughter went round the hall, for a pastoral people such as this understood the niceties of such a case. The man looked confused.

"Tell me," said Ag, "how many times has the calf trespassed on this neighbor's land?"

"O king," the man answered desperately, "I will go back to my place, and the woman being widowed of her husband may keep the calf."

The laughter swelled as the man bowed before his king, but Ag held up his hand. "Nay," he said, "for a calf is no compensation for a lost husband, and I would not have the woman hold what is yours. Go back to her, tell her it is the king's will that she restore to you your calf, and for such corn and forage of hers as it may have eaten and spoiled you shall return strict measure from your own lands. So shall both you and the woman have your own. And before you return to your place, you shall leave here with an officer of my guard, Bar-Ug by name, your own name and place, that the lord of your province may see my justice enforced."

It was a little curtain-raiser to the play that was to come, simple, patriarchal, perfect in its way—I did not wonder that Watkins longed to keep this corner of the world unspoiled, as I realised the significance of this one small incident. But I did wonder at the new dignity of Bar-Ug; he had been a simple guardsman when he returned with me.

There were no other calls for exercise of the king's judgment, and as I saw Watkins grinning his enjoyment I could hardly help laughing myself. This solitary applicant had got a verdict, certainly, but it was just as certain that the cost of complying with the conditions attaching to that verdict was more than the value of the calf. Its owner had not thought to find Ner-Ag so practised an agricultural valuer. I saw Eve's eyes sparkling with appreciation at the little comedy as she stood beside me, and there were smiles on many faces as the man bowed to the king and went his way.

When he had gone, Ner-Ag turned to the business for which he had brought this great assembly together.

"Lords and people of my land," he said, "I have called you to hear the last words that are to be said in this matter of the flight and deeds and fall of Macer, which things are known to you. If any one among you have cause to speak against that which has been done, let him speak freely and without fear, knowing that I will listen and reply justly."

He waited, but no voice answered him. Then in the simple, yet stately phrasing to which his language lends itself, he spoke his will:

"Lords and my people, all the land is at peace, and these sad things are ended. Therefore I, Ner-Ag, king, decree:

"For those who adhered to Macer there shall be no punishment other than that which has been dealt out to them before this day. Such men as remain alive shall go each to his own place, to live justly under my rule and law. And for those who served me there shall be rewards.

"For the beasts that guard the pass, such stores of food as the Nantia may ask, given freely, and for the Nantia there shall be raised a house of stone where now is her shelter. There shall be a room where she may store her food, a room in which she may eat, a room for her to sleep, and a place whence she may keep guard over the pass.

"Tain, officer of my guard, shall be governor of this city Kir-Asa in place of Neray who fled to Macer and died by Macer's hand. This reward for the man who in defeat was courageous, and in pursuit loyal and worthy of trust, my servant and my friend, and the place of governor shall be his and for his son, from generation to generation, while they hold to the law and deal justly with the people. And Bar-Ug, man of my guard, shall be officer in Tain's place, for he too served loyally and without faltering.

"And Philip my kinsman, and Jack son of Faulk to whom the hand of my daughter Eve is given, shall no longer be called strangers in this my land, but from this day shall be called the king's friends, joint lords of the western province. It shall be told throughout all the land that they two, the king's friends, are free to command the service of every man and every woman, so long as their commands be just and in keeping with the law, and they shall stand before the lords of the provinces, since their hands held the places of these lords, and my place, in the time of need. If they go to their own land, then shall my province of the west be held in trust for them, and it shall no more be called the province of the west, but the province of the king's friends. Thus shall all men know how I, Ner-Ag, king, hold all who serve, and by their service prove their fitness to rule.

"Thus I, Ner-Ag, king, decree."

We gathered, that evening, in the state apartments, Ag and his family, Watkins, Eve and I. Watkins spoke of old John's message, and expressed his intention of going to read the script before we made final preparations for leaving the country. Then he recalled the mention John had made of "emerylds."

"If I might just have a look at that necklace Eve is wearing, old chap?" he said to me.

I explained the request, and Eve took off the necklace, and handed it to him with a smile. He examined it closely.

"Have you many of these bits of green glass?" he asked Ag.

"Some few stone jars of them, yet," Ag said. "The women of the land like them strung as necklaces, and though many have been broken in the boring, many yet remain. I will bid that a jar of them, or two jars, be given you, if you will."

"In my land," Watkins told him, "this necklace would buy your place."

Ag smiled indifferently. "There must be many fools in your land, kinsman Philip," he said.

"There are!" Watkins agreed, with surprising heartiness. "Still, we will accept your gift of that jar, when we go."

"When shall we set out?" Eve asked.

Neither then nor at any other time did she show

hesitation over going. When I questioned her about leaving her family and country, always she answered simply that she had given herself to me.

"Not quite yet," I put in, and Ag smiled his approval.

Then I told her of the little Eden place down by the river bridge, that I had found when we went out after Macer.

"Before we set out on this long and perhaps dangerous journey," I said, "I want some days of rest with my princess, without the need for thought of any kind."

"Sound wisdom—we must be quite fit before we start," Watkins agreed, while Eve smiled her pleasure at the thought of our little holiday. "And you're looking fagged and played out, Jack. A quiet week or so with Eve, while I hunt round for traces of my forefather, will make a new man of you."

Then he smiled at his own inconsiderate lapse to English, and translated the sense of his words for those who could not understand them.

"I will command to-morrow," Ag said, "so that all necessary furnishings are sent to the place. It was the place of my happiest days with Niala, and you two may go when you will, to find servants waiting there to receive you with all things prepared."

I thanked him as best I could, but he made a gesture as if to put thanks aside.

"When I bade you value my gift, my Eve that is now your Eve," he said, "you bade me judge how you would value that gift, if need arose for you to render service. The need arose, and passed, and now I know that neither to you nor to Philip can I ever repay in full. Yet—we be three kings together, let us say among ourselves, and it is sad for me to think that soon I shall be king alone."

Watkins walked down with Eve and me to our house in the city, there to leave us.

"It was a good idea of yours, that of finishing the honeymoon out of the way of callers," he told me, "and seriously, too, I think you need the rest before we start."

"I'm certain of it," I said.

"Well," he advised, "take it as you took the three days I gave you. Leave everything to me for the time and when you two come back we will consider when and how to leave—and how to pack the emeralds. Eve's dowry will be something to make millionaires tremble, if we don't spoil the market by selling too many emeralds at once."

"We'll form a little syndicate," I said, "like that one for controlling the gold output from Kir-Asa when the country gets civilised. We'll unload so as to keep up the price."

"Eve," Watkins said, "when you get that man of yours to yourself, twist his ear till he howls for mercy. It will be just punishment for him."

But Eve smiled, and slipped her arm through mine as Watkins left us.

"Shall I not be good to my own?" she asked caressingly, "since ever my own is good to me?"

THE HOUSE BY THE RIVER

"No," Watkins said emphatically, "you won't take a rifle. You can have your revolver—hang it all, man, you're going for a rest with your wife, not going to war."

"I had a mind to get Eve used to the noise of a gun," I remarked. "We shall have to do some shooting when we leave, and she may as well get to know what it's like."

"Quite sound and practical," he agreed. "Take an extra twenty rounds out of the fifty Bent carried for his pistol, and blaze away at the butterflies till you're thirsty. But there's no need to make a Christmas tree of yourself with rifle and ammunition as well—you'll want the revolver as sort of precautionary measure, in any case."

As usual, I gave in. It was the morning of my setting out with Eve, and we had planned for eight clear days, exclusive of the two we meant to take on the journey there and one for return. The arrangement was to be considered elastic; we could stay longer or return sooner, just as we wished.

"Now we're on our own, Watkins," I said, "I war

to tell you the story of the place you're going to see."

Then I told him all that Tain had related to me of Eina's story.

He nodded thoughtfully. "Thanks," he said. "It would have been a bit awkward if I had butted in on the old man without knowing—he'd think it rather heartless of me to intrude on his grief, perhaps, without some word of sympathy. I'm glad you told me."

"And now," I said, "if I don't hurry, Eve will be wondering as well as waiting for me."

"I'd hate to have that happen," he answered rather ironically. "Come and let's get the good-byes over."

In spite of his inevitable irony, we had a sense of this as a memorable parting. It was the last time Ag, Niala and Ner her brother would bid good-bye to Eve as one of themselves. When we came back, it would be for an inquiet day or two before we set out to leave them for life, in all probability, and I think they saw this parting in the light of what the next would mean. In any case, before we went from the state apartments to pass through the council hall, Ag put his arm round Eve and laid his hand on her head.

"Daughter, mine no longer," he said, "I am glad in your happiness, glad you have found a man worth your love—but it will be hard to let you go from me."

"Hard for me, my father," she answered, "yet am I his, following gladly where he may lead, to make his life mine and his people mine. For my own happiness I must give all, and giving is easy where we love as I love."

Then Ag kissed her and let her go, and Niala, with tears in her eyes, kissed her good-bye. She kissed me too, for the first time, and then with a handgrip for Watkins, Ag and Ner, I got in the rickshaw that waited for me. I looked back and saw the four of them in the palace entrance, clear against the morning light that came through Kir-Asa's one priceless window behind them, and was surprised to find myself a little choky with emotion.

"Yet once more shall we see them stand thus, the three, when Philip goes with us," I said.

Eve smiled. "For this present, let us think more of the days to which we go," she answered.

167

Now happiness breeds no history, as I know, and that journey, with the days we spent in the house by the river, made greater happiness, even, than the three days that had been Watkins' wedding gift to us.

We went down the long incline from Kir-Asa, away from the straight, unwavering smoke column that went up to the sky from the volcano behind the city, leaning eastward as it rose in the slight western breeze—a faint breath, rather than a breeze, laden with the fragrance of mown grass and of the corn lands. I thought of the thousands—millions—who must have trodden this great road since the days of Kirtas-Asen and his pride, and of the mysterious second race that had risen and passed, leaving no trace beyond what we found and burned in the country palace of the kings. Had there really been a second race, or had the progenitors of this present people followed immediately on the Alantean colony? Were the wood and ivory carvings a token of their achievements before, in content and in dwindling to weakness, they suffered the arts to decay and be lost? To that questioning the long centuries hold the answer.

Down to the fertile lands, where the maize tassels shone in the fields, and the water wheels turned, as since Babylon grew and before Nineveh was a city they had turned to water the earth in eastern countries; by fields where simple, moneyless and so careless tillers of the earth paused from their tasks to look at us who passed. A smiling land, with no canker in its beauty, a land of quiet peace.

On through its gentle, slight undulations, now leaving the great road away on our right, and passing by where the cattle grazed in low-lying meadows. By reed huts where children sang as they played in the sunshine, and dark-eyed women watched our passing, until at nightfall we stayed to rest at the place that had been prepared for us. Then on through the freshness of a new day, the rickshaw wheels passing noiselessly over grassy ways till at last we ended our journey at the garden paradise beyond the river bridge, and my princess came to my arms to rest.

If I try to put into concrete incidents that last interval of happiness—for I know no other phrase that would describe it—before I left the little country where

168

Ag ruled, the incidents elude me. To attempt to grasp a love such as was Eve's and mine, to dissect it and set it down in words that some other may understand, is mere futility—I have tried once to do this, and the measure of my failure is in these pages. Of what avail would it be to try here, and to fail again?

To describe, to record? Mere futility! There would be a touch of the ludicrous if I described just how Eve tried to understand when I told her what a revolver shot is like, or recorded how she clung to my arm when I first pulled the trigger in her presence, that she might know my actual experience how the magic Watkins and I had brought to the country was no magic, but a noisy, deadly fact of everyday. Or how, in a dozen shots or more, she learned to look for the bullet's striking, and so far got the idea of magic out of her mind as to agree with me that the shot might have been a better one.

I began to teach her English; the names of common things; such words as "beautiful" and "sweet," with its variations of meaning—they were laughter-lighted lessons, for we had come to the house by the river to play like children, before facing the world, that was so new to her, as man and woman side by side. She got and used the phrase "my man" with a caressing inflection that gave the words new meaning. And, down by the bank where the garden sward sloped to the river, we found a flat-bottomed boat with a paddle and a high-backed seat for Eve—a curious craft, for the back of the seat stood up in a point like that of an ecclesiastical chair, yet not so high but that she could tilt her head back as she sat for me, standing behind her with the paddle, to bend over and kiss her lips. In this boat, when we went on the river, we kept to the shallows by the bank; out in mid-stream the current was swift and strong, and at our first venture it swept the boat a long way down until I had sense to get back close to the bank and there, out of the sweep of the deeper waters, paddle back to the garden of our desire.

Little things, these. To me, little shining threads of gold in the grey of life. Eve taught me that in a perfect love there is nothing really little, but an instant may be an eternity and one short word a song.

Thus five days fled swiftly, and at near on noon of
the sixth we sat together in our room, for the greater
heat of the day had driven us in until the sun should
have dropped some way down the sky. As we sat, Eve
pointed through the window aperture, whence the
curtain was drawn aside, and, following her pointing, I
saw a rickshaw—it may have been a mile away—coming
along the track we had followed six days before.

"Is it coming here?" Eve asked me.

"It could be to nobody else," I said. "A messenger
from Philip, perhaps, or from your father."

"He is pausing where the tracks divide," she
remarked—for there were two tracks, one that led
straight to the house, and one that wound up to the
farther end of the gardens, to come in by the servants'
quarters. "If you go to him, you may learn his message
for us the sooner."

"True," I said, "I will go."

And with a kiss for her I picked up my ammunition
belt with the revolver in its holster—for even here with
her I kept the revolver always by me—and buckled the
belt on as I went, wondering what had happened that
Watkins or Ag had sent to break in on our idyll before
the time when it should end. As I went I pointed, and
the rickshaw took the right track and came toward me.

The man within it was Bar-Ug. He leaped down and
ran toward me, and before he spoke his message his
eyes told of fear, so that I wondered what could have
happened. He stayed only to bow to me—the message
admitted of no more formalities.

"Ner-Ag, king, to you and to Eve his
daughter—return at once to Kir-Asa with Eve your
wife, and until you have her safe within the royal
palace do not for one instant leave her side. Macer,
risen from the dead, leads the things of the waste to
destroy the women of the country."

I did not answer, but turned and ran. Again I saw
Macer's limp body curved over the jutting rock, his
arms dangling down lifelessly—he must have been dead,
so to hang suspended on the hillside for so long a time.
And how came it that Ag in Kir-Asa knew of this while
we knew nothing? I overlooked the fact that we were
out of the world, voluntarily cutting ourselves off from
it for the time. And—were the things of the waste

170

potent, or was the legend of their evil power based on a mere myth?

For all these questionings, with many more that came swift as thoughts will come and pass in stress, I ran, leaving Bar-Ug to follow as he would—there was a sentence in his message which chilled me, out here away from Eve—"Do not for one instant leave her side." There was double wisdom in the command, for apart from his evil intent against the whole country, whom could Macer choose to strike with greater glee than the man who had wrought his overthrow and the daughter of the man who held his throne? I ran, the half-mile or so back to our house by the river, passed from the midday sun-glare to the cool of the central corridor, and on into the room in which I had left Eve.

She lay at full stretch on the floor, face downward, as if she had fallen thus in trying to escape from the room. Bending over her was something of which the outline was hazy and almost transparent, even in this full daylight, something indescribably hateful, revolting, demoniacal, radiating deathly evil as a fire radiates heat. As it bent down toward her still form it made the guggling, clucking noise we had heard in the place where ghosts chase women. My sight and hearing of it were momentary; I know that its outline was vaguely that of a human form; I do not even know if its head had a face; it had arms that, when I entered the room, reached down toward where Eve lay, but as I passed the threshold these arms retracted, like the eye-stalks of a snail being drawn in, but swiftly. I got my revolver loose after an infinity of pause. The thing, beast or ghost or devil, reared to a full length that was more than my own height, shortened again and swelled as might a similarly shaped mass of rubber if a weight were placed on top of it, and as I fired elongated itself in a great leap that carried it through the window aperture. As it went, either through my shot or through striking itself on the stone, it left a dull brown stain on the ledge. I rushed to the window to see it running with far more than human speed toward the trees, and as I fired again saw, not far from the point at which the flying figure seemed to aim, the face of Macer, who peered from among the shrubs. At my shot he disappeared.

171

I thrust the revolver back in its holster and turned to where Eve lay motionless and as if dead on the floor. Steps sounded along the corridor, and as I lifted Eve in my arms Bar-Ug stood in the doorway of the room.

"Search the gardens," I bade. "Macer is here."

Bar-Ug went instantly, and I was free to devote myself to Eve. She lay limp and still in my arms, and her face that a few minutes ago had told of perfect health, was deathly pale—even her lips were pale, as if all the blood had been drained from her body. I carried her over to the padded settee on which we had been seated when she caught sight of Bar-Ug, and there sat, holding her in my arms. There was a faint and fluttering pulse discernible in the artery of her neck, and she breathed faintly and lightly, as if exhausted or very ill. I could see on her no sign of violence, nor any mark; nor had the horror appeared to touch her when I came on it, though whether it had touched her before my entrance I could not tell.

For some minutes she lay still, and I heard the sounds made by the searchers in the garden as I held her. Then she opened her eyes, so slowly, and looked up at me.

"I have dreamed, dearest," she whispereed, trying to smile at me, "dreamed all the evil of the world, and that you were no longer here to hold me. So terrible a dream——"

"Rest, darling—I shall not leave you. Rest here in my arms, in your place."

"I am so cold," she whispered again, "and your clasp is so warm and strong. Kiss me, my beloved, before I sleep."

I bent my head and kissed her lips, and they were cold, so cold! She nestled closely to me as her eyelids drooped over eyes grown dim, suddenly grew rigid and shuddering, and as suddenly relaxed, with a little sigh as if she were tired, and grew quite inert. There was no longer any fluttering pulse nor any breath, for my Eve was dead.

I who have failed to tell of the splendour of her love, the glory of happiness in which Eve, living, enshrouded me—how shall I find any words to picture my despair as, with her limp body in my arms, I knew myself left desolate?

172

THE LAST PURSUIT

At some point in that day Bar-Ug was beside me, and he spoke to me. Of what he said, the one word "Macer" pierced through the numbness of my loss, telling me that there was yet a task to be accomplished. I asked, "Where is he?" and Bar-Ug pointed the way he had gone. It was down the course of the river, along its right bank—that is, the river shut him in to the western province and barred him from the fertile centre of the country between this point and Kir-Asa. He must return and cross by the bridge, or else go nearly up to the great road, if he meant to advance eastward to Kir-Asa with his terrible following, for this was the river which, winding round from the back of the volcano, swung westward for some miles and then turned to flow through the lowlands of the south before losing itself in the morasses which formed the country's boundary.

I do not know what I said to Bar-Ug, save that I bade him to see my wife's body borne to Kir-Asa, there to wait my coming. There was in my mind one clear thought, that I must go out and kill Macer. That he could not escape me, but that I should kill him, was to me as inevitable as if he waited just outside the room. Once or twice in life we meet these certainties of accomplishment, such as was this to me.

Before we left Kir-Asa, I had packed my own clothing, and it had been brought here for me. The linen clothing I had been wearing was of almost silken fineness, and I had had a thought that there might be cause to lay it aside in case of any expedition Eve and I might choose to make. Now, unhastingly, I put off the white linen and put on my own soiled and stained and shabby stuffs. There was no need for haste, for Eve was dead, and whether I set out to-day or to-morrow, Macer was mine to kill. I did not question how I should find him—I had but to follow, and knew it would be as if I were a hound following a scent up wind.

I buckled on the revolver belt, and called for Bar-Ug. "Tell Ner-Ag that when I come to Kir-Asa it will be either to bring Macer living for doom, or because I know past all question that Macer's dead body follows me."

Then, last before I set out, I went to where Eve lay as if asleep, and for a little space knelt with my head down on her breast. Once, for farewell until we two shall stand face to face beyond the stars, I kissed her on the brow, and went from the presence of her body, knowing that her spirit was with me still. But, last before I left, after the kiss that was a farewell rather to the days of our happiness than to her—for ever the sense of her presence enfolds me—I bent over and took from the still form the emerald necklace she had worn since I had first seen and loved her. This I took as the only tangible thing which should form memory of Eve—it had lain on her breast, to which her arms had drawn me, and it is round my neck now.

That last pursuit of Macer was more dream than reality, a seemingly endless going on to the accomplishment of a thing as inevitable as sunset or human death. I went as a weasel tracks down a hare, relentlessly, caring nothing whether he ran or hid or stood to fight. When I set out, one pointed—it may or may not have been Bar-Ug—and spoke some words that had no meaning for me, except that among them was Macer's name. I turned toward the way of the pointing, and left the house by the river, Eve's emerald necklace pressing, new and thus a thing in my consciousness, against my breast where her head had lain so short

More dream than reality, things and men and places growing large before me, coming abreast of me, passing behind. At times I would question, and in answer one would point, but in what shape I put the question, or who answered, I do not know. I have a memory of men wide-eyed with fear who knelt before me, the king's friend, and pointed me onward, but whether that was at the beginning or toward the end of the chase I do not know.

A memory of a little group of reed huts in the low-lying, fertile lands near the southern border, and of a man kneeling by where a woman lay dead. One pointing me onward, and the sun falling toward the western hills. I do not think I stopped to eat or drink

174

on that last pursuit. I had not eaten since Eve sat with me in the morning, but I felt no sense of hunger, nor any fatigue.

A memory of the sun having fallen within a little distance of the western hills, under whose line against the sky was blue-grey indistinctness such as the distances always show toward the day's end, as one looks toward the sun. Another woman lying dead on the ground with her man crouched beside her in still despair, and another man with hand outstretched, pointing, since the king's friend had asked the way. Yet I do not remember asking—perhaps they read my errand from my face.

A memory of guggling, hazy shapes, ever changing place and seeming to change form, and among them one figure solid and distinct, material, capable of human suffering and death. That figure fleeing away, and in the end, driven, by I know not what chance, against an unclimbable rock wall, a portion of the barrier ridge on that southern border, through which its first habitants cut the gully of the river. The things of the waste worbled and guggled in a horseshoe recess of this ridge, a curve of which the outer points were nearly half a mile apart. They were strong by reason of the dead and maniac women who marked their path across the land, and they gibbered and capered, shameless, fearless, in the light of the setting sun. Yet, dregs of the world's forming as they were, essence of the evil with which unto this day the earth is plagued, I had no fear of them; in the slow rousing from first numbness, the realisation that Eve's arms could never again in this life enfold me, I was beyond fear of the things of the waste, fearful only lest Macer should escape me.

Into this curve of the low cliff he fled with his attendant devils, looking for a path that should take him over and beyond the ridge—but there was no path. The hazy shapes drew near to him as if they looked to him for protection. As I came closer I saw him panting open-mouthed, and wild-eyed, a trapped thing that had pawned its soul and already was scorched by the flames of the hell it had made—no longer a man.

I fired one shot into the capering, guggling crowd, and the things fled all ways at the noise—they were less than child-like in their fear. They sped by me, emanating pollution as they passed, but because of the spirit of Eve that went with me they could not harm me. They left Macer alone, a trapped rat before me, ugly and fierce, turned to fight for his life at last.

He came at me from where he had shrunk back against the rock wall, barely a score yards away. I could see his teeth shining as he snarled his hate, and could see the gleam in his eyes that said he meant this fight to be his life or mine. He came toward me as his brother's spear had come in the council hall, the swift movement drawn out by a trick of my mind to an age of waiting. When he had covered a little more than half the distance, I raised the revolver and fired.

The heavy bullet, striking him below the waist, smashed his left hip joint, and he spun and fell within four yards of me. There he lay quite still, while I went and looked down at him. I recall how a little blue wisp of smoke went up from the revolver shot and melted in the sunset stillness.

I looked down on him, waiting till his foxy eyes should unclose. But when they showed they were no longer foxy, for the nearness of death brought him full realisation of the awful thing he had done in his madness. His moan was no expression of the physical pain of his wound, but was dragged from him by sight of the hell he had made, the utter impossibility of reparation, and the knowledge that he had fallen to a lower depth one more hideous, than that of the things that now fled from him back to their wastes.

"What have I done?" he moaned. "What have I done?"

But his new clarity of vision inspired me with no pity. I bent down over him, placed the revolver muzzle against his temple, and pulled the trigger. I saw the circle of burnt hair round the hole the bullet made, the shattered skull and bloody mess, and the body that quivered and presently lay quite still. Then I turned away, knowing that he could trouble the land no more.

There were men and women who clustered round, crying out to me as saviour and deliverer, and bidding me rest with them. I bade them, as the command of the king, bear the body of Macer to Kir-Asa that Ner-Ag might see with his own eyes what had come to

176

pass, and then I pushed my way through them, not heeding. I turned eastward to where the column of Kir's smoke went up into the sky, for in the city under the smoke column I should find the body of my Eve, and there would be Ag and Watkins, my friends. I pressed on, still feeling no fatigue—only a growing, clutching pain about my heart as the sense of loss grew heavier with the approach of night. Thus on until I came to the bank of the river which I must cross to go to Kir-Asa—the river on a higher reach of which was set a garden, and the house where Eve and I had loved. These waters that hurried past had flowed by the Eden of our desire.

Here was moored to the bank such a boat as that in which Eve had sat with head flung back. Here, without going up the stream to find a bridge, was means of crossing to go on to Kir-Asa. I stepped into the boat, took up the paddle, and cast off the rope that held the craft to the shore. A warning cry came from beyond the bank I had left, but I took no heed.

The nose of the boat swung out toward mid-stream, and I plied the paddle to send it across to the farther bank—it was in my mind, then, to get up from the river valley to higher ground, so that I might see a course to steer before the light failed. Then suddenly it was as if a hand took hold on the prow of the boat and flung it violently to point down stream. The tremendous force of the current tore the paddle from my hand, and I was helpless in a current that swung me onward to the southern border at the pace of a horse's gallop.

The sun had just set, but still the earth was lighted. I saw the land where I had won and lost so much slip past, caught one glimpse of the even line against the sky that I knew was the hewn wall about Kir-Asa the mighty, and saw the pillar of smoke go up from Kir. I knew this for the end, and, save for the thought of Watkins, was almost content.

The ridge of rock that formed the border of the fertile lowlands for miles, here in the south, rose before me ere the light died out from the sky. I saw in the ridge a yawning cleft, square-cut, that looked like a precipice edge, or like the brink of a waterfall, for it formed a sky-line as I approached it. As this came before me in the day's last gleam, the boat shot forward as if propelled by human agency at a faster rate than the tearing current of the stream. And now I was on the brink, now over—Kir-Asa was lost to me.

There showed a reach of nearly a mile of river running at an angle between smooth-cut rock walls, down the slanting channel that had been hewn through this ridge when the world was young. The surface of that reach was dark and smooth, without a ripple, like a sheet of deeply-stained glass, yet so fast did the waters flow in their smooth-cut bed that I felt the wind in my face as the boat sped down—was it minutes or only seconds that I endured the mad, silent rush through the changing of day with night? I recalled that, back in Kir-Asa, Watkins had spoken of how we three should go down this silent torrent, Eve and I together, and himself at the steering oar.

I heard a roar ahead, saw dimly a boil of white foam at the end of the hewn incline—I saw this dimly because of the mist that came before my eyes at thought of how Eve had planned to share this peril with me. I stood up in the unguided craft as the roar grew louder, peered ahead at the broken water where the river fell to level, and as the boat's prow struck on the boiling surge I was flung forward—I remember my chest striking the high back of the seat like that one on which Eve had sat. . . .

PERHAPS

And that happened just three months ago.

There were two men, named Carr and West, who had heard of an oil seepage in the marsh lands. They took guns and quinine, and a party of twelve bearers, and set out to scour the marshes, but they found no oil. At one dawn, in a little creek of almost stagnant water, they found a quaintly-built boat with its gunwale almost awash, and in the boat was a senseless and nearly dead man whom they took to their camp and nursed back to consciousness.

I remember looking out as I lay in the shelter they made for me, and seeing, very far off and faint to the north-eastward—so far off, and so faint against the skyline—a pillar of smoke that went up and feathered

178

out at the top like the foliage of a palm. So far off, and so faint. . . .

They were very good to me, these two men. I lay in the shelter they made for me, and they kept to their camp for three days because of me. After that, as I grew no better, they made the bearers improvise a stretcher on which to carry me. My chest was bruised black, and there was some internal injury that caused a grating feeling when I moved, while from time to time I would spit up gouts of blood. Yet there was not overmuch pain. West judged that when the bruise on the chest was made I must have broken a rib or two, and the jagged edges of bone had penetrated the coating of the lungs. Carr said that if this were so, I should be dead. Finished with their prospecting, they determined to carry me to a mission station. . . .

Now, since all this is ordinary, everyday experience, I have no intention of relating it in detail, beyond showing that these two men were as kind and considerate as men could be. They tended me on the long, weary journey like trained nurses, and in the end we came to the mission station, to find in the missionary—he lived there along with a staff of native helpers—one of those rare, fine men God makes sometimes to give the rest of us faith in our kind. He knew something of medicine and surgery, as do most of his craft, and he told me that though there would be a boat bringing his letters in about five weeks' time, he would not advise me to attempt the journey to civilisation until the boat after that, unless I really wanted to kill myself. Carr and West, who wanted to go off to the westward to prospect some more marsh lands for oil, told me that they would be compelled to miss that first boat in any case, and would see me safe to my journey's end on its successor.

Now, for my own peace of mind's sake, I wanted to send some word of Watkins to the outside world, and in thinking how this might be done I remembered that, when we made the contract that took us to Kir-Asa, he had given me a cheque on a bank in Singapore, the name of which I knew. I wrote a letter to the manager of the bank, asking him to forward the enclosure to the nearest relative of Philip Watkins, who had an account with him—or to the nearest relative whose name and address he knew.

Then I set about writing the enclosure. At first it took the form of a long letter, but the few details of our journey I could include even in a very long letter made an utterly preposterous and incredible story, so that after two or three attempts I gave it up, and wrote the story out in full. Now, when Carr and West return, they will take this manuscript to Singapore, and hand it with its covering letter to the manager of Watkins' bank. In a separate envelope will be enclosed a sketch map I have made, to show where we landed from the tramp steamer to begin the journey to Kir-Asa. And whatever he or she may do with the manuscript, I trust that the recipient of it and the map will hold the map as secret, understanding that in writing I have kept in mind how Watkins and I promised each other that we would keep the garden land of Kir-Asa a secret from the world, that not through us should civilisation be let in to spoil it.

For my own peace I must send this message to his kin-folks, that, if they so will, they may go or send to find him. If they will not do this, still they may know that I, who am proud to have been his friend, have placed on record for them this portion of the life of a very brave and courteous gentleman, friend of a king whom he made in a city older than any on earth.

Often I wonder about him. Did he make a great search for me, when the bodies of Eve my wife and of Macer who compassed her death came to Kir-Asa the mighty, or did he know, through the one who uttered that warning cry as I pushed out to be caught by the current of the river, how it was that I did not return? Did he in the end take the stone jar of emeralds, gift of Ner-Ag, and with it go down the gully of the river that sucked me out from Ner-Ag's land, or did he go the way of the place where ghosts chase women and the great gorge of the trembling bridge? Or does he perhaps still stand beside the king of his making, his kinsman and friend, by the carven throne of stone that is in the council hall of the king's palace, away in the hewn city of wonder? However these things may be, I feel that he is not dead. Somewhere, in his own inimitable way, he is fighting life, and I would that I might grip his hand and stand beside him.

Thus at times, when he is much in my thoughts, I question. It may be that in the end I shall go back to Kir-Asa to see if he is still there. And then again I feel that sight of the city of wonder, of Ag's kindly face, and the sound of voices speaking the language in which my princess talked with me, would bring too keen an ache. It may be that I shall go back to Watkins—I do not know. In any case, I shall not return to England. I have nothing of great worth except Eve's emerald necklace, and that will be buried with me when my time comes. For me it has a greater value, since when I knew my princess it lay on her breast.

Carr and West will take this manuscript and the map to Singapore, and I shall not go with them. Yet perhaps I shall not go back to seek for Watkins, after all. This last week or two I have known myself not so strong, and yesterday the haemorrhage from my chest began again. The missionary has just been in for one of his cheery talks, but to-day he seemed not so cheery as usual. He said nothing definite, this good man whose care has been more than I can ever repay, but I gather from his manner—which is almost pitying—that I may, perhaps, go out beyond the swing of the tides of earth, to where is waiting my Eve with the shining eyes and arms outstretched to clasp me at my coming. I can still recall the tender note in her voice as she told me she would wait for me, beyond the stars. It may be—and this in reality I desire most—that her waiting is near its end.

I have told such a tale as has never been told, and in sending it on think that the Watkins who receives it will see its truth in its linked inevitability. If thus he sees it, and if I go to Eve, it is for him to find his kinsman, my friend, should he wish. As for me, life had its real beginning when first I took Eve in my arms, and now, lying here with the story told, I realise that it ended for me when I laid my princess down.

A NOTE BY THE RECIPIENT OF THE MANUSCRIPT

This manuscript was forwarded to me from my cousin's bankers in Singapore, but the map of which mention is made in its concluding pages was not enclosed. I have been unable to find any trace of oil prospectors named Carr or West, and it may be noted that the missionary who is spoken of as having taken charge of Faulkner is not mentioned by name, while the manner of writing the story is such as to give very little clue, even to one who knows the Pacific archipelagoes, to the precise direction in which to search for the coast on which my cousin landed with his companions. Also, unfortunately, the old diary of which mention is made in the story is no longer in existence. Otherwise, it might have been possible to find traces of my cousin from the directions contained in it. Although for over two years I have caused the most diligent search to be made, and inquiries set afoot in every possible way, so far there has been no satisfactory result.

It is beyond question that my cousin was in Penang with two men named Bent and Faulkner nearly four years ago, and none of the three has since been heard of. Publication of this manuscript may lead to discovery of the name of the boat by which they left Penang, or to that of the missionary (though this I think unlikely, since in all probability he will never see the story) or of the men Carr and West.

LEONARD S. WATKINS

THE END